THE NOTEBOOK OF DOOM

COLLECTION

SUBJECT

Three Books in One!

by Troy Cummings

BRANCHES

SCHOLASTIC INC.

To Penny and Harvey: Stay out of trouble.

To Professor Klaus: Good luck to you in your various undertakings.

To Mom:
Thanks for having me!

Thank you, Katie Carella and Liz Frances, for taking my ideas
and making them better.

Copyright © 2013 by Troy Cummings

All rights reserved. Published by Scholastic Inc., *Publishers since 1920.* SCHOLASTIC, BRANCHES, and associated logos are trademarks and/or registered trademarks of Scholastic Inc.

The publisher does not have any control over and does not assume any responsibility for author or third-party websites or their content.

No part of this publication may be reproduced, stored in a retrieval system, or transmitted in any form or by any means, electronic, mechanical, photocopying, recording, or otherwise, without written permission of the publisher. For information regarding permission, write to Scholastic Inc., Attention: Permissions Department, 557 Broadway, New York, NY 10012.

This book is a work of fiction. Names, characters, places, and incidents are either the product of the author's imagination or are used fictitiously, and any resemblance to actual persons, living or dead, business establishments, events, or locales is entirely coincidental.

ISBN 978-1-338-10199-7

10 9 8 7 6 5   20

Printed in the U.S.A.   23
First printing 2016

Book design by Liz Frances

THE NOTEBOOK OF DOOM COLLECTION

TABLE OF CONTENTS

Book #1: RISE OF THE BALLOON GOONS   1

Book #2: DAY OF THE NIGHT CRAWLERS   95

Book #3: ATTACK OF THE SHADOW SMASHERS   189

THE
NOTEBOOK OF
DOOM

SUBJECT

RISE OF THE BALLOON GOONS

NO. 1

Troy Cummings

SCHOLASTIC

TABLE OF CONTENTS

Chapter 1: STERMONT   3

Chapter 2: FRIGHT AND EARLY   6

Chapter 3: MAP OUT OF IT!   10

Chapter 4: ONE-TWO PUNCH!   18

Chapter 5: A TON OF BRICKS   23

Chapter 6: GOING DOWN!   32

Chapter 7: THE MORGUE THE MERRIER   36

Chapter 8: SPILLED MILK   43

Chapter 9: MONSTERS BEFORE BED   52

Chapter 10: ~~HAPPY~~ BIRTHDAY   57

Chapter 11: A REAL TWIST   63

Chapter 12: CLOWNING AROUND   68

Chapter 13: *PSSSHHHHH!*   71

Chapter 14: BOUNCING OFF THE WALLS   74

Chapter 15: READY OR KNOT   80

Chapter 16: THE POINT   84

STERMONT

Once there was a pile of bones.

Actually, the bones weren't in a pile. They made up a small skeleton, which was filled with squishy guts. On top of that skeleton sat a huge skull with deep eye sockets. These eye sockets held a pair of googly eyes.

The whole thing would have been really gross, except it was covered in a layer of skin and had a mop of curly hair on top. This mop-haired, bug-eyed, gut-filled bag of bones was named Alexander Bopp. And he was scared to death.

Alexander was scared of:
1. spending his first night in a new house;
2. going to a new school in a new town; and
3. having to make new friends.

Alexander rolled over on his air mattress and looked out the window. The moon lit up a row of rooftops, behind which stood a water tower that said STERMONT. Alexander's new home.

2 FRIGHT AND EARLY

Alexander's dad drove slowly down Main Street. "I'll look on this side, and you look on that side. This town must have a breakfast place."

Alexander looked out his window. They passed a park, a bank, a comic-book shop . . . and then someone dancing like crazy on the sidewalk. Wait, it wasn't a person. It was one of those bendy balloon guys that businesses put out to attract customers. It was yellow, and it was

wiggling beside a sign that said
NOW SERVING BREAKFAST!

"Hey, Dad," Alexander said.
"Here's a place."

They parked next to
the dancing balloon guy.

NOW
SERVING
BREAKFAST!

7

"Whoa!" Alexander jumped in his seat. The balloon guy had flopped right onto the windshield. It snapped back up and continued to dance.

Alexander's dad shook his head. "You're jumpy today, Al. That's just a big bag of air."

"I know," said Alexander, uncovering his eyes.

"In fact," said his dad, "we should be happy to see this goony-balloony. Otherwise we might have missed this diner." He made a dopey face and wiggled his fingers at the balloon figure. "Thanks, balloon goon!"

Alexander smiled. Then he walked the long way around the balloon and into the diner.

3 MAP OUT OF IT!

The door chimed as Alexander and his dad left the diner. "Were those great pancakes, or what?" his dad asked.

Alexander didn't answer. He was studying his paper place mat: a map of Stermont, laid out like a maze.

"Hey, neat," said his dad. "Maybe we could take extras to hand out at your party."

Alexander poked his nose over the map. "Party?"

"Sure!" said his dad. "Your birthday party!"

"But, Dad," Alexander grumbled, "I don't want a party. I don't even *have* a real birthday this year."

"But that's the best part about a leap-year

birthday, Al," said his dad. "February twenty-ninth only comes around once every four years. So we get to *choose* your birthday this year. And I choose tomorrow!"

Alexander frowned.

"Besides," his dad continued, "I already made the party invitations." He stuffed a stack of envelopes into Alexander's backpack. "Pass 'em out to your new classmates today!"

Alexander followed his dad toward their car. Way down the street, he could make out a wiggly shape in front of a bank — another dancing balloon guy. This one was purple.

"Hey," said Alexander. "There's another" — he looked around — "wait … where's *our* balloon goon? It was right here when we parked. . . ."

NOW
SERVING
BREAKFAST!

"*Hmmm?*" said his dad. He was fishing around for his keys. "I dunno. Maybe someone moved it." He unlocked the car. "Hop in, Al!"

Alexander tried to yank open his door, but then — CRUNCH! — it scraped against the curb. "Huh?" he said. The car was lower to the ground than before.

"Dad! This tire's flat."

"No problemo," said his dad. "We'll just pop on the spare and — wait a minute! *This* tire's flat, too." He rubbed his chin.

Alexander took a step back. "Uh, Dad. All *four* tires are flat."

"That's strange," said his dad. "Maybe there's glass on the road. . . ."

Alexander looked across the street: two more cars with flat tires. *Something weird is going on here*, he thought.

His dad stood up and brushed off his pants. "Sorry, Al. I have to call a tow truck. Do you think you could walk to school?"

Alexander's eyes widened. "By myself?"

"Sure, kiddo!" His dad smiled. "Here — pass me that place-mat maze."

His dad spread out the place mat on the hood of the car and pulled a pen from his pocket.

"See — we're here," he said, circling the diner. "And your new school is right there."

He drew a path through the maze. "You head down Main Street and — oops, dead end! Turn left and then north and then — oh! We got stuck in the glue factory! Wait, wait. So you loop back — oh, wow! This town has three graveyards! And then you go past that bakery. And bingo! You're at school!"

Alexander gulped. *My first day in a new town,* he thought. *And I'm walking myself to school.*

"Now go make friends. Then tomorrow we'll have a birthday blowout! High five!"

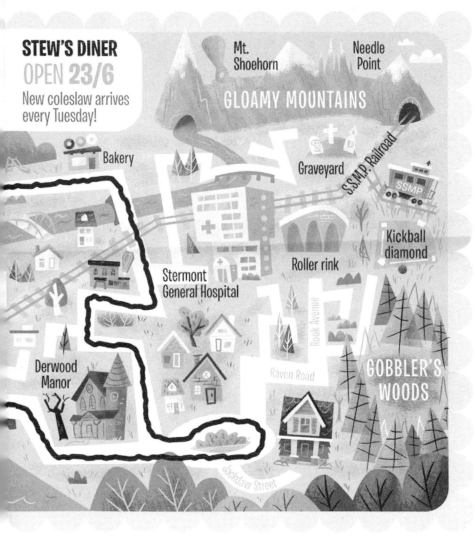

Mt. Shoehorn

Needle Point

GLOAMY MOUNTAINS

Bakery

Graveyard

S.S.M.P. Railroad

SSMP

Kickball diamond

Roller rink

Stermont General Hospital

Rook Avenue

Raven Road

GOBBLER'S WOODS

Derwood Manor

Jackdaw Street

Alexander gave his father a medium five. Then he followed his place-mat maze down Main Street.

CHAPTER 4 ONE-TWO PUNCH!

A lexander soon found himself at Stermont Elementary. There was no one else around. *I must be late,* he thought.

He headed toward the door — but then froze. Two balloon goons were wobbling there — one blue and one green.

Alexander took a big deep breath. As he stepped between the balloons, he saw words printed on them. The blue balloon said PARDON, and the green one said OUR DUST. Alexander looked down but didn't see any dust.

There was a tug on his backpack. He looked over his shoulder and saw a flappy blue arm tangled in the straps.

Alexander untwisted the wiggling arm and turned to see . . .

. . . the green balloon goon's big, ugly face!

"Whoa!" Alexander shouted. The goon's nose pressed right up against Alexander's.

Then — FOOMP! Alexander was clobbered on the head, from behind. It felt like he'd been socked by a boxing glove. He spun around just in time to be hit in the face. FOOMP! Alexander stumbled and fell backward.

Both balloons leaned over Alexander, grinning. Their long, wobbly arms swooped in and grabbed at his jacket. Alexander tried to kick them away, but the green one wrapped its arm around his ankle. Alexander's shoe came off as he tried to wriggle free.

KER-SMASH!!!

A loud crashing sound came from inside the school. The balloon goons instantly let go of Alexander. They snapped upright.

Alexander scrambled to his feet and ran into the school. His heart was pounding as he yanked the door shut behind him.

5 A TON OF BRICKS

Alexander stood inside, catching his breath. The school was perfectly quiet, and all the lights were off. Daylight came in through the door behind Alexander, casting long shadows down the hallway.

"Hello?" he called out.

"Hello?" said his echo.

Alexander clutched the straps on his backpack and started down the dim hallway. He passed several classrooms, all empty.

"Anyone there?"

Alexander tripped over something brown with white stitches. *A flat football . . .* he thought.

CRASH-BLASH KER-SMASH!

A brick wall collapsed in front of him. A cloud of dust filled the passage, covering Alexander like a powdered donut.

Alexander looked through the broken wall and saw a giant yellow claw — a wrecking crane!

He *had* to get out of there. He climbed over the smashed bricks, which was tricky with just one shoe. Then he spotted something rectangular in the rubble, wrapped in a dusty scarf.

Alexander unwrapped the object. It was an old notebook.

He flipped to a page in the middle.

PLAYING MANTIS

A huge green bug monster. About as tall as a giraffe (minus the neck).

HABITAT All playgrounds — at schools, public parks, etc.

SNIFF! Rainy days make the playing mantis sad.

DIET Regular-size bugs. (They spit out the shells.)

BEHAVIOR These giant bugs love playground equipment, but they play too rough. If you notice a dent in the slide or see a swing with one chain shorter than the other, then there's likely a mantis nearby.

WARNING! The only way to avoid a playing mantis is to sit quietly against the wall during recess.

Alexander shivered. He thumbed through the book and saw page after page of monster drawings.

"HEY!" a voice shouted from down the hall.

Alexander stuffed the notebook into his backpack.

A woman was storming toward Alexander. She wore a gray shirt, gray pants, gray shoes, and gray glasses. Her hair was in a long braid, coiled on top of her head like a snake.

"Why are you playing in a construction site?!" she demanded.

"I wasn't playing! This is my school. I'm a

new kid! But nobody was here and then the wall crashed and —"

"This school was closed to deal with —" The woman looked at Alexander.

"Well, this is a dangerous building," she continued. "Even a 'new kid' should have been able to read the warning sign out front."

"Do you mean the big 'Pardon Our Dust' balloons?"

"Balloons?" asked the woman. "No. There's a big 'Danger! Keep Out!' sign, Alexander."

Alexander blinked. "How did you know my name?"

The woman smiled. Actually, she didn't smile; she just frowned less. "We've been expecting you. Only we expected you at the *right* building. Not the one being torn down."

Alexander pulled out his map. "But it says here —"

The woman snatched the map away. "This place mat is outdated! We've moved the school while they finish construction." She reached into the coils of her braid and pulled out a marker.

"You're here," she said, circling the school. "And your new school is . . . here." Ignoring the maze, she drew a line that cut through someone's backyard and a funeral home, ending at **STERMONT GENERAL HOSPITAL**.

She handed the map to Alexander. "Now get to school, before your principal gets angry."

"My principal?" asked Alexander.

The woman knelt down. Her ID badge dangled before Alexander's eyes.

STERMONT ELEMENTARY

MS. VANDERPANTS
PRINCIPAL

Ms. Vanderpants waved for Alexander to get moving. So he did.

Alexander looked up at the hospital. Right away, he noticed how *this* Stermont Elementary was better than the other one:

    1. The lights were on.

    2. It hadn't been knocked over by bulldozers.

A man sat at the front desk, writing on a clipboard. He had frizzy white hair that stood straight up. Alexander read the nameplate on the desk.

MR. HOARSELY
SECRETARY

"Excuse me," said Alexander.

"*Eep!*" Mr. Hoarsely said. "You scared me!"

"Sorry," said Alexander. "I'm new here, and, uh . . ."

"Oh, you must be *Alexander.*" Mr. Hoarsely checked his clipboard. "Well, look at that . . . happy sort-of-birthday."

He checked his watch. His eyebrows shot up. "You're late! And filthy! And why are you only wearing one shoe?"

FEBRUARY
28

"Stermont Elementary students *must* wear both shoes at all times — school policy!" said Mr. Hoarsely. He pulled a pair of green galoshes out of the Lost & Found. "Quick — put these on before the principal sees you!"

Alexander took the galoshes. They looked like little froggies.

"I can't wear these!" he said.

"Ms. Vanderpants will flip if she sees a sock-footed student!" said Mr. Hoarsely.

Alexander made a sour face and pulled just the left galosh over his sock.

"Perfect. Now, let's find your class," said Mr. Hoarsely, checking his clipboard. "Sixth graders are in the Emergency Room....Kindergartners are in Brain Surgery.... Ah — here you are!"

He pointed to the elevators. "Press  M to get to your classroom."

Alexander stepped into the elevator and pressed M.

The elevator went down several floors and then opened. Alexander read the sign on the wall:

Morgue? thought Alexander, stepping out of the elevator. *But that's where hospitals keep dead bodies!*

CHAPTER 7
THE MORGUE THE MERRIER

Alexander tugged open the big metal door and peeked into a cold, windowless room.

The walls were lined with little square doors. Most of the doors were open, with long metal slabs sticking out like tables. Alexander's new classmates were using these slabs as desks. The class grew silent as Alexander stepped into the room.

"WHO DARES ENTER THE FORBIDDEN CHAMBER?" boomed a loud voice.

One of the square doors in the back of the room shuddered and then burst open.

"AHHH!" Alexander screamed.

A grinning man had popped out of the hatch. "Ha! Just kidding! Welcome! I'm Mr. Plunkett!" He wore a pink-and-orange flowery shirt, green pants, and purple shoes.

Mr. Plunkett wrote ALEXANDER BOPP on the board. Then he plopped a pointy hat onto Alexander's head. "Why don't you introduce yourself?"

"Um, hi, I'm new and it's great to meet you and my dad is a dentist and we just moved to Stermont yesterday and, um —" Alexander said, way too fast.

The classroom door swung open with a big jerk. Rip Bonkowski barged into the room.

39

RIP BONKOWSKI

Spiky hair

Square-ish head

Missing teeth
Baby teeth? Or did he lose them in a fight?

Fake tattoos

"Who's the weenie?" Rip asked, staring at Alexander.

"Now, Rip," said Mr. Plunkett. "Is it a good idea to call someone a 'weenie'?"

Mr. Plunkett turned to the class. "Remember what we talked about in our writing unit! You can call *anyone* a weenie — so boring!" He winked at Alexander. "If you're going to give someone a nickname, make it count!"

Alexander's mouth dropped open.

"Let's see. . . ." Mr. Plunkett studied Alexander. "Notice his silly frog boot. This guy clearly loves slimy green things!"

He crossed out Alexander's name and wrote SALAMANDER SNOTT beneath it.

"There!" he said.

The class broke into laughter.

Alexander tore off his hat. "Unbelievable!" he snapped. Everyone stopped laughing. "A lousy nickname already? This whole day has been a joke!" Alexander gritted his teeth. "I've been lost, yelled at, crushed by bricks — and attacked by monsters!" He held his hands up like claws. "Huge, ugly, terrible, walking balloon goons!"

Everyone gasped. Then they laughed even harder. Except for a hoodie-wearing kid in the back row. He or she scribbled something in his or her notebook.

"Oh, Salamander," Mr. Plunkett said through tears of laughter, "you are one *funny* fella!"

Alexander shook his head. *Why did I just tell everyone about the balloon goons?* he thought. *Good thing I didn't mention the monster notebook!*

"Speaking of funny," said Mr. Plunkett, "I'd like to discuss a little prank I found on my seat." His eyebrows lowered.

Mr. Plunkett slapped a deflated whoopee cushion on his desk.

WHOOPEE!

"A *flat* whoopee cushion is no joke," he said. "Next time, fill it with air!"

RRRIINNGG!

The class rushed past Alexander. *Finally, lunch! This day is bound to get better*, he thought. *Right?*

CHAPTER 8 SPILLED MILK

Alexander took the elevator to the cafeteria. **DING!** The doors slid open.

FOOMP! Alexander was hit in the face with a dodgeball.

"Gotcha, Salamander!" said Rip.

The ball landed with a thud at Alexander's feet.

"Oh, man! It's flat," Rip said. "I was hoping to bounce it off your nose!"

"Ripley Bonkowski!" came a voice from around the corner.

"Uh-oh," said Rip.

Ms. Vanderpants thundered into view.

"Alexander," she said, "I see you made it to school."

Alexander nodded.

She turned to Rip. "Take a seat. Now." Rip shot Alexander a mean look. Then he sat down. Alexander breathed a sigh of relief and got in the lunch line.

MENU

	MONDAY	MEAT LOAF SURPRISE
	TUESDAY	SQUASH SURPRISE
	WEDNESDAY	CHILI SURPRISE
	THURSDAY	LIMA BEANS (NO SURPRISE)
	FRIDAY	TACO SURPRISE

He grabbed some Taco Surprise and looked for a seat. Most of his classmates were eating together, joking around. The kid in the hoodie sat alone, writing in a notebook.

The notebook, remembered Alexander. He found an empty table, unzipped his backpack, and pulled out the notebook. It was filled with drawings of monsters — hairy birds, eight-eyed mushrooms, mutant earthworms.

He read about flying rhinos while he ate.

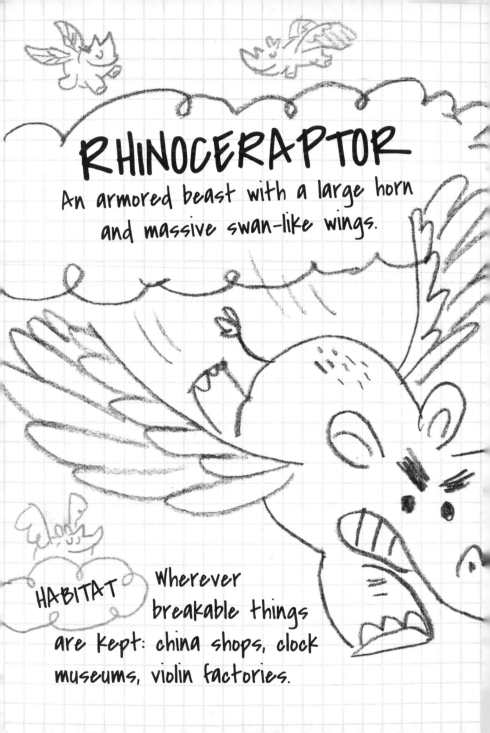

RHINOCERAPTOR

An armored beast with a large horn and massive swan-like wings.

HABITAT Wherever breakable things are kept: china shops, clock museums, violin factories.

YUK-YUK! Rhinoceraptor feathers are great for tickling your enemies.

> DIET Leafy plants. And corn dogs.

> BEHAVIOR These monsters enjoy a peaceful life in the clouds. But if they spot something breakable down below, they immediately dive-bomb their target!

> WARNING! Stay calm! The rhinoceraptor can sense fear, so, SERIOUSLY, DON'T FREAK OUT!

The rhinoceraptor won't hurt you, but it'll gladly crush anything you care about—like a fishbowl, a sand castle, Mr. Nuzzle Bear, or a picture of your mom.

Alexander finished his lunch and closed the notebook, bumping his milk carton. It was 2% milk, but 98% of it splashed onto his pants. He began dabbing milk off his pants with his napkin. Then he paused mid-dab.

There was a message on his napkin.

I KNOW ABOUT THE MONSTERS.

It looked like the message had been signed. But the name had been smudged by spilled milk.

Alexander felt a hard slap on his back.

"Hey, Salamander," said Rip, pulling up a seat.

Alexander jammed the notebook into his backpack. "Stop calling me that!" he said.

"What are you trying to hide?" asked Rip. His hand shot down into Alexander's backpack.

"That's mine!" said Alexander.

Rip smiled. "What's this?" He pulled out a baby-blue party invitation:

Who's a **BIG BOY?**

Come to a **birthday party** and find out!

WHERE? 55 Jackdaw St.

WHEN? Saturday morning!

WHY? To make new friends!

"Hey, everybody!" Rip announced. "Salamander Snott is having a birthday party tomorrow! Looks like he's turning two!"

"No!" Alexander stood up. But then he remembered the wet spot on his pants. He sat back down.

Rip marched around the lunchroom, holding up the card.

Alexander felt a gentle pat on his back.

"Here —" said a girl's voice.

It was the kid in the hoodie. She wore the hoodie pulled way, way down. But Alexander could see she had friendly eyes.

"For your pants," she said. She handed him a paper towel. "Hey, I saw your notebook earlier. I keep —"

A buzzer sounded from the loudspeaker.

BWAAAMP! BWAAAMP!

"Er, hello, students," said a voice. "This is Mr. Hoarsely. School has been cancelled."

"Yeah!" shouted Rip as he high-fived a kindergartner on the head.

The speaker crackled again. "The tires have gone flat on all the school buses. Ms. Vanderpants has called off afternoon classes today so you have plenty of time to walk home."

Everyone looked to the teachers' table. Mr. Plunkett was clapping.

"Flat tires on every bus?" he said. "Now, *that's* a prank!"

The students filed out of the cafeteria. Everyone was excited to be walking home on their own. Everyone except for the filthy, tired, frog-booted kid with wet pants.

9 MONSTERS BEFORE BED

lexander watched his classmates head off in different directions. The hoodie girl was nowhere to be seen. *Could she have slipped me that note?* he wondered.

On his walk home, Alexander saw one balloon goon — an orange cactus. A group of older kids walked right past it. The balloon danced around, but they didn't seem to notice.

Was I really attacked *by balloons this morning?* thought Alexander. *Maybe the monsters in that weird notebook are getting to me.*

Alexander couldn't wait to look more at the notebook. He hurried the rest of the way to his new home: a small yellow house on the edge of town, near Gobbler's Woods.

"I'm home!" called Alexander. He kicked off his mismatched shoes.

His dad was unpacking dishes. "How'd it go?" he asked.

"Um, okay," Alexander said.

Alexander ate dinner and got ready for bed. It felt good to wash up and change into clean pajamas. He climbed onto his air mattress and, at last, brought out the notebook.

What could S.S.M.P. stand for? he wondered. *And these monsters . . . are they just some kid's doodles? Or could they mean something?* He read another entry.

S.S.M.P.

DOOM!

FORKUPINE

A small metal rodent
with a coat of tiny, sharp forks.

HABITAT Most forkupines prefer dry climates. But the stainless-steel forkupine can be found near rivers, lakes, or in the back of dishwashers.

CLANG!

Magnets will not work on forkupines.

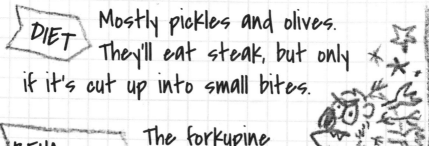

DIET Mostly pickles and olives. They'll eat steak, but only if it's cut up into small bites.

BEHAVIOR The forkupine stays sharp by rubbing against a brick wall.

WARNING! Never pet a forkupine! Instead, lure it to a plate of spaghetti. (Forkupines LOVE rolling around in noodles!) This will give you time to sneak away.

FUN FACT The forkupine is a distant cousin to the sporkupine. But the sporkupine's scoop attack is no match for the forkupine's jab.

"Okay, kiddo, lights out!" Alexander's dad peeked in the door. "Big day tomorrow! I can't wait to see who comes to your party!"

"Uh . . . me neither," said Alexander. He faked a yawn and let his blanket fall onto his backpack, still full of invitations.

10 ~~HAPPY~~ BIRTHDAY

"U*rggghh!*" Alexander woke up with a sore back. His air mattress was flat. *Like the dodgeball,* he thought. *And the tires . . .*

Alexander's dad was outside, singing at the top of his lungs.

Alexander looked out the window. His jaw dropped.

HAPPY BIRTHDAY TOOOOO YOUUU!!!

His front yard was full of balloon goons! Every size, every color. All of them grinning up at Alexander.

His dad was in the middle of the group, singing like a rock star.

Alexander waved his arms. "Dad! No! Get out of there!" he cried.

His dad looked around, confused. "What?"

"THOSE . . . GOONS! THEY'RE GONNA GET YOU!"

His dad laughed. "Oh, Al, there's nothing to be afraid of. I called Party Planet yesterday to rent something fun for your birthday — it's set up out back! And then this morning, these balloons were waiting in our yard. The store must have thrown them in for free!"

"Those things are monsters!" Alexander shouted.

Alexander's dad sighed. "Al, they're not monsters." He strolled through the yard, bopping balloon goons. He even stopped to honk one on the nose.

"See?" he said. "Now, come downstairs and let's party!"

Alexander got dressed and headed downstairs.

At first glance, Alexander thought his dad had turned the backyard into a birthday wonderland.

HAPPY BIRTHDAY, AL!

HAPPY BIRTHDAY!

But then Alexander noticed the melting ice cream, the droopy party balloons, and a nervous clown. *Yikes!* thought Alexander. *Good thing I didn't actually invite anyone to this party!* Even the main attraction — a bouncy castle — looked like a smooshed tent.

"*Hmmm,*" said Alexander's dad. "That castle was fully inflated a minute ago. Maybe it's got a leak. . . . I'll check it out. You go on and say hello to your friend."

Friend? thought Alexander. He turned to see a square-headed kid carefully making his way through the front yard. The one person to show up at his party: Rip Bonkowski.

Alexander frowned and walked toward Rip.

CHAPTER 11
A REAL TWIST

"All right, Rip, get it over with," Alexander said. "Throw something at me or call me names or whatever, so you can go home."

"Sounds like fun," Rip said, "but that's not why I'm here. I actually came to tell you" — he slurped some punch — "that I believe you. About the monsters."

Alexander was speechless.

"Did you *hear* me?" asked Rip.

"So, wait," Alexander said. "Are *you* the one who wrote on my napkin yesterday?"

Rip looked confused. "Napkin? No. I thought you were nutso then. But as I was walking home from school, I passed by one of those balloon things. A big orange cactus. It gave me a funny look, so I started throwin' rocks at it. It caught one of my rocks and threw it back at me! Look!"

Rip rolled up his sleeve. There was an ugly red scrape between some of his fake tattoos.

"Whoa," said Alexander.

"Yeah," said Rip. "And then the thing started chasing me! I ran home. I tried to tell my parents, but they didn't believe me. I still had your stupid invitation in my pocket, and I remembered what you'd said in class. So I came here."

Rip rolled his sleeve back down. "Your front yard is *crawling* with those things! I had to sneak around them."

"Who can we tell about the balloon goons?" said Alexander.

They looked at the two grown-ups at the party: Alexander's dad, who was fussing with the bouncy castle, and the nervous clown.

"Let's try the clown," Alexander said.

Alexander and Rip walked over to the clown.

The clown wore a fake bald cap and big, pointy shoes. A smile was painted on his face, but he didn't look happy. He was blowing up a balloon.

"Excuse me," said Alexander.

"Eep!" The clown released his balloon. He glanced at the woods, then back at the boys. "Pay attention!" he said. "I'm about to show you a very important balloon animal."

"Um, okay . . ." said Alexander.

The clown blew up a long, skinny balloon.

"Now watch!" He held the balloon by one end and twisted the other end around. "Left, right, left. Down, around, pull!"

He gave the balloon one last tug. "Ta-daaa!"

"What is it?" asked Alexander. "One big knot?"

"No — a mangled pretzel!" said Rip.

The clown wiped his brow. "Just remember: left, right, left. Down, around —"

"Hi, boys!" Alexander's dad jumped out from behind a shrub.

"Eep!" the clown shrieked, dropping his balloon knot. The balloon popped and the clown shrieked again.

Alexander's dad laughed. "This guy's a hoot!"

"Yeah, he's crazy all right," said Alexander, peering into the woods.

12 CLOWNING AROUND

I've got terrible news," said Alexander's dad. "I can't get this bouncy castle all the way aired up."

He pointed to a poster on a nearby tree. "But here's something even better: Pin the Tail on the Donkey!" He held up a cardboard tail attached to a long, sharp pin.

"That looks dangerous!" said the clown, taking a step back.

Alexander's dad removed his tie. "Nope!" he said. "Here. Blindfold me — I'll show you!"

The nervous clown tied the blindfold. Then Alexander's dad spun around three times. He smiled and began marching in a straight line . . . away from the donkey.

"Dad —" Alexander said.

"I can do this!" his dad said. "Watch the master."

Alexander, Rip, and the clown all watched Alexander's dad walk across the backyard and around the corner of the garage.

The clown tugged nervously on his suspenders. "Maybe we should practice more balloon animals until your dad comes back."

Rip elbowed Alexander in the ribs. "Tell him, Salamander."

"Um, Mr. Clown," said Alexander, "you know those balloons in my front yard?"

"Yes?" he said.

"I know this sounds crazy," Alexander said, "but Rip and I" — he leaned in — "we think they're alive. They're monsters!"

"I believe you, Alexander. I'm the one who wrote on your napkin."

"Huh?" said Alexander. "Wait, *you* were at the cafeteria?"

The clown looked straight at the boys. "And even if I didn't believe you before," he whispered, "*Ummm* . . . Turn. Around. Slowly."

Alexander and Rip turned. A white balloon goon was dragging itself along the ground. It was floppier than the others.

The clown's makeup turned two shades paler.

"Their secret is in these woods, behind your house." The clown was backing away. "They'll do anything to protect it. RUN FOR YOUR LIVES!"

Alexander watched as the clown jumped out of his shoes and ran, faster than any clown has ever run from a balloon.

PSSSHHHHH!

The white balloon goon lurched toward the two boys.

"Rip, run!" Alexander shouted.

"No," Rip said. "It's just a balloon." He picked up a giant clown shoe. "I say we fight."

Alexander scrambled onto the picnic table.

The balloon goon opened a large valve on the bouncy castle. Air rushed out with a great PSSSHHHHHH! The goon chomped on the valve, swelling up from the escaping air.

"It's eating the air," Rip said.

"It all makes sense now!" yelled Alexander. "The flat tires, the dodgeball, my mattress — these goons have been stealing air from everything in town!"

The balloon goon had doubled in size. It had four wiggly arms, all reaching for Rip.

Rip held the floppy shoe like a baseball bat. "You don't scare me."

The goon scrunched down like a spring and then vaulted toward Rip. Rip swung the pointy-toed shoe with both hands — SPLACK! — making a tear in the goon's silky belly. The monster collapsed as the air whooshed out of its wound.

Alexander shouted down to Rip. "You did it!"

Rip twirled the shoe on the end of his finger. "Of course I did, Salamander."

Then one hundred more balloon goons came to the party.

CHAPTER 14 BOUNCING OFF THE WALLS

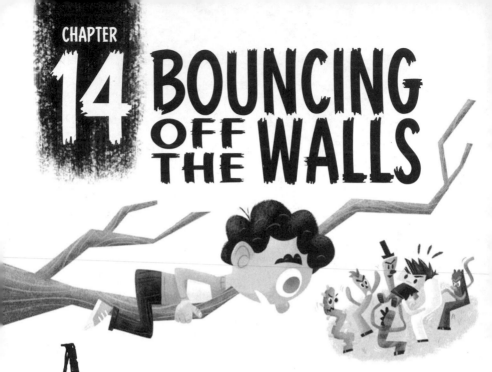

Alexander climbed up onto a nearby tree limb. "C'mon, Rip!" he yelled, climbing higher.

Balloon goons filled the backyard. The group from the front circled around the house as dozens more glided in from the woods. The crowd of swaying monsters silently zeroed in on Rip.

"No way!" said Rip.

He swung his clown shoe but was no match for the balloons. They grabbed Rip and lifted him high in the air.

"Salamander! Help!" he shouted.

Alexander hugged his branch as the balloons carried Rip off into the woods.

A moment later, Alexander dropped from the tree.

WHO WILL SAVE RIP?

Alexander's dad? **NO.** Wandered off wearing a blindfold.

The nervous clown? **NO.** Ran away crying.

Stanley the Steam Shovel? **NO.** Imaginary cartoon character.

Alexander? **YES!** The only one around.

Alexander trailed the balloon goons as they marched through the woods. Then he gasped.

Before him stood the largest bouncy castle ever built! It was the size of a real castle, with towers, battlements — even a drawbridge. Except the entire thing was made of rubber.

The balloon goons dragged Rip into their bouncy fortress, leaving the drawbridge open.

Alexander stepped onto the drawbridge. It wobbled slightly. He took a breath and entered the gate.

It was dark inside. Alexander could hear a faint SHHH-SHHHHH sound, as though the walls were breathing. There was no sign of Rip or any balloon goons.

Walking was tricky, so Alexander tried jumping. The springy floor launched him up to the ceiling. He rebounded off a wall and bounced down the hallway.

Alexander bopped his way through the maze of passageways. He got lost a few times but eventually found himself in the heart of the fortress. It was an enormous room with no ceiling — just the blue morning sky.

In the middle of the arena, a kid was tied to an inflatable post.

Alexander leaped over. "Rip! You're alive!"

Rip smiled. "Salamander! Untie me!"

Alexander worked at the knots. "Why did they bring you to their fortress?"

"Fortress?" Rip snorted. "This place is a *factory*! While you were playing hopscotch, they brought out a million baby balloon goons and forced me to blow 'em up. Once I ran out of breath, they tied me up."

"Is that their secret?" Alexander asked. "They're building an army?" He loosened one knot, but there were dozens to go. "Just imagine: no pool toys! No bikes! And" — he swallowed — "no whoopee cushions! We *have* to stop them."

The ground began to quiver. Alexander heard a low rumbling, like hundreds of basketballs being dribbled at once. An army of angry balloon goons swarmed in from all sides.

The boys were surrounded.

15 READY OR KNOT

Hold still!" said Alexander.

"It's no use," said Rip. "There are too many knots!"

More balloon goons were pouring into the room. Alexander had to think fast. He jumped straight up, came back down, and then bounced higher. He came down a second time and a third, until he shot up above the tallest goons. They wobbled in place, their eyes fixed on the leaping boy. Alexander bounced higher yet. From way up there, the goons looked small — harmless, even.

"Heads up!" shouted Rip.

Alexander saw the green OUR DUST balloon from the corner of his eye. It twirled something on the end of a string and let it fly.

WHAP!

Alexander was hit by his old shoe, and began to fall. He hugged his knees and cannonballed into the crowd. He slammed down onto the green balloon goon.

That goon exploded, releasing a blast of air that knocked the rest of the goons to the floor.

"That," said Rip, "was amazing."

Alexander shakily stood up. "We can take 'em. One at a time, they're not very strong."

"Uh-oh . . ." said Rip. "Look!"

The floored balloon goons were crawling toward one another like inchworms. They began twisting their bodies together and had soon braided themselves into one gigantic balloon snake.

The massive snake reared its head high, casting a shadow on the boys.

16 THE POINT

Alexander's eyes grew wide as the giant balloon snake towered overhead.

"So. About these knots —" said Rip. **FWISH!** The snake wrapped itself around him.

Knots, thought Alexander. His eyes lit up. "Rip, don't move."

"No problem," Rip squeaked.

"Hey, airhead!" Alexander shouted at the snake.

The snake turned to face Alexander. Then it attacked!

Alexander bounced to the left, dodging the snake's head.

He frog-hopped around the arena, changing direction with each leap.

"Left! Right! Left!" he shouted. The snake followed Alexander's lead.

Alexander sprung off a wall and flew behind the snake. "Down! Around!"

Finally, he landed near the snake's tail and rocketed straight up. "PULL!"

The snake's head shot through its own coils, stretching its body tight. Its huge jaws snapped at Alexander but missed. He fell to the ground and then looked up. The snake had let go of Rip. It had tied itself into a knot — a giant copy of the clown's balloon animal!

The snake began twisting about, trying to untangle itself. But the more it struggled, the tighter it squeezed, until . . .

BLAM!

. . . it exploded into a shower of confetti.

Alexander ran over to untie Rip. Then the two boys bounced their way out of the fortress.

Rip looked at the mop-haired, bug-eyed, gut-filled bag of bones that had saved his life. "Thanks, Alexander."

Alexander grinned. "My friends call me Salamander."

"You know," Rip said, "anyone brave enough to take on an army of —"

SSSSHHHHHH! The boys turned around. The bouncy fortress had sprouted arms, legs, wings, and a long, spiky tail. It had turned into a huge balloon dragon!

The dragon charged at the boys.

The dragon
zoomed up into
the sky like the
world's loudest
whoopee cushion.
A blindfolded man
stood where the
balloon dragon had
been. He was holding
a long, sharp pin.

"Did I win?" asked
Alexander's dad. He peeked under his
blindfold. "Nuts! Not even close!"

The boys laughed. "I could really go for some
cake," said Alexander.

PFFFT!

They hiked back to the party. Alexander's dad studied the donkey poster while the boys headed to the picnic table. They found the clown hiding underneath. His bald cap had fallen off, revealing a shock of white hair.

"Mr. Hoarsely!" Alexander said. "*You* passed me that note?"

"Boys — you're not dead!?!" said Mr. Hoarsely.

Rip flexed his muscles. Alexander rolled his eyes.

Mr. Hoarsely climbed out from underneath the table. "Does this mean you know about the *other* monsters?" he asked.

Rip looked around. "Other monsters?"

"Hang on!" Alexander ran inside and brought out the notebook.

Mr. Hoarsely trembled. "How did you find *that*?" He leaned in. "Yes. As you can see, those balloons were only the beginning. If you're smart, you'll —" He looked up.

Alexander's dad was standing there.

Mr. Hoarsely shook Alexander's dad's hand. "Thanks for hiring Clowns-to-Go. Gotta go!" He gave the boys a serious look. They could tell he had more to say, but that it would have to wait.

"What did he mean by 'only the beginning'?" Rip asked.

Alexander whispered, "Can you keep a secret?" He handed the monster-filled notebook to his new friend.

Rip flipped through a few pages. "These monsters aren't scary," he said.

Alexander poked Rip's shoulder. "Before today, would you have thought *balloons* could be scary?"

"Good point," said Rip. "Hey, why are there empty pages in the back?"

Alexander held up a pencil. "I think I know." He turned to the first empty page and began to write. . . .

BALLOON GOON

A tall, wiggly creature that is full of air. Most people pass right by these monsters without giving them a second glance.

HABITAT Balloon goons dance in front of used-car lots, diners, and construction sites. They sometimes build balloon fortresses where they can hang out.

SIZE CHART

KID   GOON

SHHH! Balloon goons are totally silent creatures.

DIET A balloon goon eats air that it steals from things like footballs, whoopee cushions, and air mattresses.

BEHAVIOR

An army of balloon goons can twist together to form a giant balloony snake monster!

WARNING! Carry a pin if you think a balloon goon is nearby. They'll really get the point!

THE NOTEBOOK OF DOOM

QUESTIONS & ACTIVITIES!

Look at the map on pages 16-17. Make a map of your town. Include your home, school, and spooky places.

Adjectives describe nouns. For example, *tall*, *spooky*, and *bumpy* are adjectives. List 3 adjectives to describe the balloon goons.

On pages 66-67, Mr. Hoarsely shows Alexander how to make a balloon animal. How did the balloon animal help Alexander free Rip from the gigantic balloon snake?

How do balloon goons compare to monsters from other books?

Create a new monster! Give it a name. Draw and write about its **habitat**, **diet**, and **behavior**. And be sure to add a **WARNING!**

TABLE OF CONTENTS

Chapter 1: A NICE, WORM BREAKFAST — 97

Chapter 2: RAIN, RAIN, ^DON'T GO AWAY — 102

Chapter 3: DIAL *H* FOR HOARSELY — 108

Chapter 4: RETURN TO SENDER — 112

Chapter 5: *SCREEEECH!* — 118

Chapter 6: TABLE FOR THREE — 124

Chapter 7: SWORD OF A BIG DEAL — 127

Chapter 8: IN THE LOOP — 134

Chapter 9: FISHING FOR ANSWERS — 138

Chapter 10: DIG IT! — 145

Chapter 11: CLASH BEFORE CLASS — 148

Chapter 12: FLOP QUIZ — 151

Chapter 13: ON THE WRONG TRACK — 156

Chapter 14: HARD TO SWALLOW — 161

Chapter 15: SLIP OF THE TONGUE — 170

Chapter 16: *BLAAARF!* — 180

A NICE, WORM BREAKFAST

"Look out, Al. . . . Here comes a monster!"

"Where?!" cried Alexander. A week ago he would have thought his dad was joking. But now, after moving to Stermont, he couldn't be sure. This town was packed with monsters.

"RARRR!" Alexander's dad said, handing him a plate. "A *breakfast* monster!"

97

Alexander sighed.

"Sorry there's no mouth on this breakfast monster, but I didn't have any bacon," said Alexander's dad. "Now chow down! I have to fetch the newspaper before it floats away!"

Alexander glanced out the window. It was pouring.

CLACK. As soon as Alexander heard the front door close, he pulled a beat-up notebook out of his backpack.

The old notebook had a creepy-looking skull and the initials *S.S.M.P.* on the cover. Alexander had been studying this notebook ever since he'd found it. The book was full of drawings and facts about monsters.

Alexander wasn't sure who had started the notebook, but last week he'd written his own entry after defeating an army of balloon goons. Alexander could still hardly believe that the dancing, wiggling, arm-waving balloons were actually monsters!

Alexander snapped the book shut as his dad came back in, sopping wet.

His dad tossed a soggy newspaper onto the table.

STERMONT NEWS

GRADE SCHOOL CONSTRUCTION UNDER WAY

PLOP!

Drops of water splashed onto Alexander's plate, along with something long, pink, and wiggly.

"Yuck — a worm!" Alexander yelled.

"It's just a night crawler," said Alexander's dad.

Alexander put his fork down. "I think I'm full now," he said.

Alexander stuffed the notebook into his backpack. "I should get to school," he said. "I'm walking with Rip." At first, Alexander had thought Rip was a bully. But now they were friends.

"Okay, Al. Stay dry!" His dad mussed his hair.

Alexander opened the front door. The storm clouds made everything seem gray — except for the ground. The ground was sort of pinkish.

As Alexander stepped out onto the front porch, he could see why.

Everywhere he looked —
his yard, his driveway, the
sidewalk — little pink night
crawlers were wriggling.
Thousands of them.

"Ugh," said Alexander.
The only thing squirming
more than the worms
was his stomach. He
opened his umbrella
and headed out.

BOPP

2 RAIN, RAIN, DON'T ↑ GO AWAY

Alexander tiptoed down the rainy sidewalk.

He made his way to a playground where his friend Rip was sloshing around.

"Hey, Salamander!" Rip shouted.

Salamander was Alexander's nickname, whether he liked it or not. He sort of liked it.

"Wanna see something gross?" Rip asked. He raised a boot over one of the squirming worms.

"Rip, no!" said Alexander. "Don't!"

Rip lowered his foot a little. "They're just worms! What's the big deal?"

Alexander sighed. "Rip, when we fought those balloon goons, we helped

everyone in Stermont — even these tiny worms. If we go around squishing 'em, we're no better than the monsters we were trying to stop!"

Rip made a gagging sound. "Fine," he said. "But it's weird to be surrounded by worms. I feel like a meatball wading in spaghetti!"

"You're right, Rip." Alexander's eyes grew wide. "This *is* weird. Super weird!"

He pulled the notebook out of his backpack.

"The notebook!" Rip said. "Hey — what does S.S.M.P. stand for, anyhow?"

"I don't know yet," said Alexander. "But look! There's something in here about worms!"

MEGAWORM

A small blue worm that seems harmless. At first.

HABITAT Megaworms can be found on wet ground and sidewalks.

BEHAVIOR Megaworms always travel alone.

DIET Unknown. Possibly eats kids.

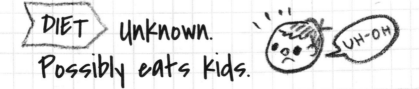

UH-OH

POP! Megaworms smell like caramel corn.

WARNING! A megaworm starts out tiny, but grows bigger than a school bus when sunlight hits it. Keep megaworms out of the sun!

BEFORE   AFTER

WEAKNESS Any kind of loud screeching sound makes them shrivel up.

"This can only mean one thing," said Alexander. "These night crawlers must be megaworms!"

"Yeah . . ." said Rip. "Wait — no! That notebook says megaworms travel alone." He pointed the umbrella toward a nearby heap of worms. "There must be *millions* of these guys. There's no way they're megaworms!"

"But what if you're wrong?" asked Alexander. "What if all of these worms grow huge and start eating kids?!"

Rip shrugged. "The monster notebook also says megaworms are blue — but these worms are pinkish gray!"

Alexander held up a finger. "Then let's do a test!" he said. "A screech should shrivel them up." He squatted down near a worm, took a deep breath, and —

AAAR GHGH GHH!!

The worm wiggled a little.

Rip tugged at Alexander's elbow. "C'mon, Salamander. Let's get to school."

"Well, okay . . ." said Alexander. "Maybe Mr. Hoarsely can tell us about these monsters. Remember what he said at my birthday party?"

"Yeah," said Rip. "He said that those balloon goons were only the beginning."

"I just wish we knew what he meant. . . ." said Alexander.

CHAPTER 3
DIAL *H* FOR HOARSELY

SWISH! The Emergency Room doors opened as Alexander and Rip entered the old hospital building, which was now their school.

A tall man with tall hair was leaning on the front desk. He was putting on a pair of sneakers.

"Mr. Hoarsely!" Alexander called. "Worm monsters are attacking Stermont!"

"Maybe," Rip added.

"SHHH!!" Mr. Hoarsely said, looking around.

108

"I *know* there are monsters here, but the worms —"

"Right — the worms!" said Alexander. He gave Rip an I-told-you-so look.

"I'm sorry," Mr. Hoarsely said. "I need to make an announcement." He picked up a microphone.

"Testing . . ." he said. The speaker on the wall was silent. He flipped the switch to INSIDE. "Good morning, students." His voice sounded shaky. "Since it's such a rainy and, uh, wormy day, we'll be having gym indoors."

INSIDE

OUTSIDE

"Okay, Mr. Hoarsely," said Alexander, "what about these megaworms? If we don't stop them before the sun comes out, they'll —"

"Look," Mr. Hoarsely said, putting a whistle around his neck, "I'll see you in gym class. I really need to —"

BRRRINGGG!

"Eep!" Mr. Hoarsely jumped. He picked up the phone. "Stermont Elementary, no longer Stermont General Hospital. May I help you?"

Alexander whispered to Rip, "Gym class? Wait — isn't Mr. Hoarsely the school secretary?"

"Yeah," Rip said, "but he's also the gym teacher, the nurse, and a bus driver. The school is saving money by —"

"WHAT?! NO!" Mr. Hoarsely screamed into the phone. "I'm not going to fight *you*!"

Alexander glanced at Rip. Rip shrugged.

"NO!" Mr. Hoarsely lowered his voice. "Um, could you hold?" He pressed the HOLD button.

"Boys," Mr. Hoarsely said, staring dead ahead, "get to class." He hunched over the phone and returned to his call.

"But if sunlight hits those worms, Stermont is toast!" said Alexander. Rip shook his head and dragged Alexander toward the elevator.

The sky outside was still cloudy. For now.

4 RETURN TO SENDER

WORMS!

Alexander and Rip walked into their underground classroom, which used to be the hospital morgue. Now instead of being a place for storing dead bodies, it was a place for storing bored students.

"If it isn't the Tardy Boys!" said a short man wearing three kinds of plaid.

"Morning, Mr. Plunkett," Alexander said to his teacher.

He found a seat in the back, next to a girl in a hoodie. She was the only kid who had been nice to him on his first day of school.

"Um, hi," Alexander said.

She was busy reading a book and didn't seem to hear him.

Alexander took out his monster notebook and flipped to the megaworm pages. *How can I stop them?* he thought.

The hoodie girl turned her head a little.

Is she peeking? worried Alexander. He quickly turned to a different page to hide the megaworm pages.

KOALA-WALLA-KANGA-WOMBA-DINGO

Ears of a koala

Snout of a dingo

Claws of a wombat

Pouch of a kangaroo

Tail of a wallaby

HABITAT These monsters are found beneath the bathroom sink. Or below the couch cushions. Any place that's down under.

FLOOSH! Toilets flush counterclockwise when K.W.K.W.D.s are nearby.

DIET Boomerang-shaped food: bananas, croissants, squash, etc.

BEHAVIOR Koala-walla-kanga-womba-dingoes love to cuddle.

WARNING! It's a trap! As soon as you touch a koala-walla-kanga-womba-dingo, a joey will pop out of her pouch and nip your nose. Anyone bitten by a joey instantly becomes Australian.

Alexander closed the notebook. *Too bad we're not under attack by cuddly koala-kanga-whasits,* he thought. *I'd take those over megaworms any day.*

"Students," said Mr. Plunkett, "today's lesson will be entirely about worms." The hoodie girl was opening her science book.

Alexander jotted a note on a scrap of paper, folded it, and handed it to the hoodie girl.

"Pass this to Rip," he whispered.

She nodded and sent the note along. After a few passes back and forth, their conversation filled the page.

We've got to stop these monster worms before the sun comes out! –Alexander

THEY'RE PROBABLY NOT EVEN MONSTERS! –RIP

What if I'm right, though? I need to make a loud screeching noise to make the worms shrivel up. I can do it – with Mr. Hoarsely's help. But I have to do it *now*! –Alexander

SO DO IT ALREADY! —RIP

But how do I get out of class? -Alexander

Just ask for a bathroom pass! -Nikki

STAY OUT OF THIS, NIKKI! Salamander, just ask for a bathroom pass. -RIP

Alexander sat upright. *"Nikki?"* he said aloud.

The girl next to him tugged on her hoodie strings.

"Excuse me, Alexander," said Mr. Plunkett. Everyone turned to look. "Do you have something to say?"

"Um, I, yes —" Alexander glanced at Nikki and Rip. "I've got to go to the bathroom. It's an emergency!"

Mr. Plunkett scratched his mustache. "Okay. Come get a hall pass. You've got five minutes!"

Alexander took the hall pass and ran. He knew just what he had to do. . . .

Like a secret agent in sneakers, Alexander crept through the empty cafeteria. Some lunch ladies — and a lunch man — were busy cooking something green with purple chunks.

Or is it purple with green chunks? thought Alexander.

A small blackboard hung on the wall.

MENU	
MONDAY	CHEF'S CHOICE
TUESDAY	CHEF'S 2nd CHOICE
WEDNESDAY	LEFTOVERS OF CHEF'S 1st CHOICE
THURSDAY	CHEF'S NEXT-TO-LAST CHOICE
FRIDAY	THE CHEF HAD NO SAY IN THE MATTER.

Alexander took down the blackboard.

Okay, he thought. *I just need to bring this to Mr. Hoarsely and —*

DING! The elevator doors slid open.

Alexander dove behind a fake fern, almost dropping the blackboard.

"— and here we have the last part of our tour: the cafeteria," said Principal Vanderpants.

Alexander peeked over the fake fern. Ms. Vanderpants came out of the elevator, followed by a masked woman in padded clothing.

"Terrific," said the masked woman. Or maybe she had said "Jurassic." Her voice was muffled by the mask.

"I'm pleased you could fill in on such short notice," said Ms. Vanderpants. "It's unlike Mr. Hoarsely to just disappear."

MR. HOARSELY
SECRETARY

Disappear? thought Alexander.

The two women walked into the cafeteria. Alexander clutched the blackboard and slipped into the elevator just before the doors closed. He pushed **1** for the first-floor lobby.

DING! Alexander burst out of the elevator.

He looked out the lobby window: The ground was carpeted with night crawlers. The sky was still overcast, but the clouds were thinning out.

He sprinted to the front desk. "Mr. Hoarsely! I need your —"

Alexander stopped short. The desk was a mess. Papers were scattered about. The phone was off the hook. And Mr. Hoarsely was not there.

Alexander picked up the receiver. "Hello?"

Silence.

Alexander hung up the phone.

Mr. Hoarsely has *disappeared,* he thought. *And it looks like he left in a hurry!*

The room brightened. A sunbeam broke through the clouds, shining on the worms below.

"No!" Alexander lunged across the desk and grabbed the microphone. "Take this!" he yelled, raking his fingernails across the blackboard.

SCREEEEECH!

A terrible sound thundered through the building.

Oops, thought Alexander. The microphone was still set to INSIDE.

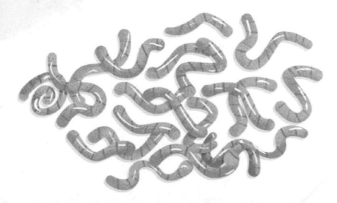

DING!

The elevator doors slid open. "Alexander!" Ms. Vanderpants rushed out. "We do not *play* on the intercom!"

Alexander quickly flipped the switch to OUTSIDE and scratched the blackboard again.

SCREEEEECH!

He looked out the window. The night crawlers were now bathed in sunlight. But they just kept wiggling. None of them grew as big as a school bus, and none of them ate anyone.

I was wrong, thought Alexander. *They're just plain old worms.*

He relaxed a little. "Everyone's going to be fine," he said.

A firm hand squeezed his shoulder.

"I don't think *everyone's* going to be fine," said Ms. Vanderpants. "My office. Now."

CHAPTER 6 TABLE FOR THREE

By the time Alexander made it to lunch, the cafeteria was out of green stuff. They were just serving purple chunks.

He took a seat next to Rip.

"That was a super-long bathroom break," Rip said, winking.

"Yeah, Ms. Vanderpants was pretty mad," said Alexander. He sniffed a purple chunk. "You know, I've never been in trouble like that before."

"You get used to it after the first six or seven times." Rip chugged his milk. "So . . . About those worms . . ."

"Okay, okay — you were right," Alexander grumbled. "They were just regular night crawlers."

"Poor Salamander . . ." Rip smiled. "It must be hard being friends with a smart guy like me!"

Alexander swallowed a mouthful of chunks. "I was wrong about the worms, but there *are* more monsters in Stermont. Mr. Hoarsely said —"

"Monsters? What are you two talking about?" Nikki set her tray on the table and sat down.

"None of your business," Rip growled. "Now bug off!"

Nikki turned to Alexander. "So, how did everything go with the worms?"

"Uh, fine." Alexander frowned. "I guess."

They all stared at the table.

"Lunchtime is over," Rip said, glaring at Nikki. He turned to Alexander. "Let's go, Salamander. I'm sure Hoarsely will fill us in during gym."

"Oh!" said Alexander "I almost forgot — Mr. Hoarsely is missing! I overheard Ms. Vanderpants telling some weird lady about it."

"Really?" asked Nikki.

"He probably got spooked by his own shadow," said Rip. "I bet he's hiding in a locker, waiting for gym class to start."

"I sure hope you're right," said Alexander. "I've got a lot of questions for him."

CHAPTER 7
SWORD OF A BIG DEAL

STERMONT ELEMENTARY
A. BOPP

W ait up, Rip!" said Alexander as he pulled on his gym shirt.

Alexander walked into the gym. Actually, it wasn't a gym — it was a hospital laundry room.

Students had lined up near a row of washing machines. Everyone wore matching gym clothes, except for Nikki. She joined Alexander and Rip at the end of the line.

"You wear your hoodie to gym?" Alexander asked.

"Yes." Nikki jammed her hands into the hoodie's pockets. "I have a . . . condition."

"What do you mean?" asked Alexander.

CLANG! CLONG!

The students stopped talking. "What was that?" someone whispered.

Alexander pointed to a square hole in the ceiling. "It's coming from the laundry chute!"

BUMPA-BUMPA-BOOM!

"Is someone up there?" asked Nikki.

"Duh, Nikki!" Rip sneered. "I bet that chute is Hoarsely's hidey-hole!"

The clanging sound grew louder until — **WHOOSH!** — a white blur tumbled through the chute. The blur caught a water pipe and flipped backward through the air,

landing perfectly on its toes.

Whoa! Alexander took a step back. It was the masked woman he'd seen earlier.

The class started clapping.

"She's an acrobat!" said Nikki.

"Acrobat, nothing," said Rip. "She's a *ninja*!"

The woman took a bow.

"Good afternoon, students. I am Coach Gill." Her voice sounded wet and bubbly, like she was gargling mouthwash. "I'll be filling in while your teacher is . . . on vacation."

Alexander raised his hand. "But Mr. Hoarsely isn't —"

Coach Gill leaped across the room and landed in a crouch, inches from Alexander.

"Yes?" She read Alexander's shirt. "Mr. Bopp? Were you going to correct me on the whereabouts of" — she took a raspy breath — "Mr. Hoarsely?"

Alexander stared into Coach Gill's face mask, but all he could see was darkness. He also caught a whiff of her breath. *Pee-yew! Someone had tuna for lunch!*

"Um, no," he said, leaning back. "Never mind."

Coach Gill stared at Alexander a moment longer.

"Today," she said, "you will learn the sport of warriors — fencing!"

She wheeled out a laundry cart full of swords. "Everyone, take a practice foil," she said. "Once you've sharpened your skills, you may one day use a real blade. Like mine."

Alexander tapped Rip's shoulder. "Doesn't her sword look weird?"

Practice foil
(Short and flimsy)

Coach Gill's sword
(Long and sharp)

Rip didn't answer; he was busy swishing his foil around. "This is so cool! I can't believe we're sword-fighting!" he yelled.

Coach Gill flicked her sword — **CLACK!** — knocking Rip's foil to the floor.

"It's *fencing*, not sword-fighting," she said.

"Everyone, watch." She jumped up onto a laundry-sorting table. "Stand like this. And hold your foils like this."

The students waggled their foils.

"Terrible!" Coach Gill screamed, looking directly at Alexander. "You've got 24 hours to shape up. There'll be a quiz tomorrow. CLASS DISMISSED!"

8 IN THE LOOP

After school, the sky was still partly cloudy and the ground was still partly wormy.

"There are fewer night crawlers than before," said Alexander.

"You're right," said Nikki. "I wonder where they — *oof!*"

She had stumbled over a mound of dirt.

"Watch out for molehills," she said, pointing to a second dirt pile.

Rip walked behind Alexander and Nikki, swinging his practice foil. "It's so awesome we get to take our swords home!"

Alexander rubbed his chin. "Don't you think Coach Gill is kind of . . . strange?"

"No way!" said Rip, slicing at the air. "She's great!"

"But what about her mask?" asked Alexander. "She never takes it off — even outside of class."

"Coach Gill is a *professional!*" Rip lowered his foil. "You wouldn't understand, unless you were into sword-fighting."

"You mean *fencing*," said Nikki.

"Eat worms, weirdo!" Rip yelled.

"Guys! Stop!" Alexander said. "Look!" He pointed to the sidewalk. Dozens of night crawlers had twisted themselves into a loopy squiggle.

"Whoa," said Rip. "It's some kind of secret code."

"That's no code," said Alexander. "It's fancy lettering! The worms are writing something." He squinted. "Can you guys read cursive?"

"Nope," Rip said. "They don't teach cursive at Stermont Elementary."

"I can read it," Nikki said.

"What?" Rip snapped. "If *I* can't read it, then neither can you!"

"Sure I can," Nikki said. "I learned cursive *years* ago."

Rip cocked his head. "Years ago? Baloney! That's —"

"Great!" said Alexander, putting a hand on Rip's shoulder. "So, Nikki, what are the worms trying to tell us?"

Nikki peered at Alexander from under her hood. "Beware! The fish are coming!"

The fish are coming!

Despite the night crawlers' weird warning, Alexander, Rip, and Nikki all had to get home for dinner.

Alexander dropped his backpack as he came in the door.

"Son?" said his dad. "Have you been battling fearsome enemies?"

"Dad — I can explain! Those balloon goons were —"

"Balloons?" His dad chuckled. "I was thinking pirates — or musketeers!" He pointed to Alexander's backpack.

Alexander exhaled. "Oh, that!" He yanked out his practice foil. "That's just homework."

He bounded up the stairs. "Call me when dinner's ready!"

Alexander sat down at his desk and made a list of questions and clues.

1. WHERE IS MR. HOARSELY?
   -He got a scary phone call.
   -He left in a hurry.

2. WHAT DOES S.S.M.P. STAND FOR?

3. WHO IS COACH GILL REALLY?
   -She got mad when I mentioned Mr. Hoarsely.
   -She won't take off her mask.

4. HOW COULD WORMS WRITE A MESSAGE?

5. WHAT DOES "THE FISH ARE COMING" MEAN? ? ? ? ? ?

The fish . . . thought Alexander. *Wasn't there something about fish in the notebook?* He turned past the mostly ripped-out first page and began thumbing through the book.

He stopped at a page filled with fish. *This is it!* he thought.

TUNNEL FISH

A creature that can "swim" underground. It drools A LOT, which loosens the dirt, making it easy to dig.

SIDE EFFECT Tunnel-fish slobber makes night crawlers super smart, allowing them to read and write.

TEE-HEE! Tunnel fish have ticklish tongues.

HABITAT Dirt, soil, mud. Not cement.

DIET Anything smaller than itself. When tunnel fish are near, worms flee to the sidewalks for safety. Tunnel fish will sleep for 99 years after a big meal.

WARNING! Don't get tunnel-fish drool on you — it's super-gross!

Tunnel fish! thought Alexander. *Tomorrow, I'll —*

"Dinnertime!" called Alexander's dad.

Alexander ran downstairs. His mind was racing so much he could hardly eat his pizza.

"All right — all done!" Alexander said, wiping his mouth.

"Hold on," said Alexander's dad. "I've got a surprise for you. Catch!" He tossed a round red object across the table.

Alexander caught it. "A yo-yo?"

"Yep!" his dad said. "Yo-yos are prizes for my patients — to reward them for flossing. Neat, huh?"

"Yeah," said Alexander. "Well, good night!"

He headed upstairs, tossing the yo-yo into his backpack on the way.

Unfortunately, Alexander was so excited about the tunnel fish that he forgot to floss.

CHAPTER
10 DIG IT!

Ha! Take that!" Rip yelled, practicing his fencing moves.

"Hey, Rip!" Alexander called, running over. "Look what I found last night." He opened the notebook. "The worms were warning us about monsters called tunnel fish!"

"Wow," Rip said, reading the page. "So the worms popped up to avoid becoming tunnel-fish bait?" He looked down. "But wait—that means fish monsters are tunneling under us *right now!*"

A dirt pile nearby trembled. Something underneath burrowed straight for the boys.

Alexander stepped back. Rip drew his foil.

POP! A purple fish burst from the ground. It had spiky fins, mean-looking eyes, and a mouthful of teeth. It would have been terrifying, except it was the size of a pickle.

The tunnel fish chomped a worm near Alexander's foot and then dug back underground.

Rip sneered. "Tunnel fish are weenies! We can just smoosh 'em!" He stopped sneering. "Hold on, Salamander . . . what's *that*?"

Another dirt pile rumbled and then —
SPLOTCH! A silver tunnel fish — the size of a dolphin — shot out of the ground. It swallowed the purple fish in one bite and plowed back underground.

Alexander gulped. "I guess they come in all sizes," he said.

The boys looked at each other and took off running.

11 CLASH BEFORE CLASS

LAUNDRY
GYM

ow do we fight the tunnel fish?" Rip asked, catching his breath.

"I don't know," said Alexander.

"*There* you are!" said Nikki. She had been pacing outside the gym. "I've been looking for you all morning, Salamander. I —"

"Don't call him *Salamander*!" Rip said through clenched teeth.

Alexander gave a little wave. "Uh. Hi, Nikki."

Nikki turned to face Alexander and Rip.

"I've been watching you," she said. "I know there are monsters in Stermont, and I know you've been fighting them. Last night, I was chased by a fish-creature the size of an alligator!"

Alexander's mouth hung open.

"So what?" said Rip.

Nikki sighed. "So let's work together! I've got some useful, um, skills. And I've been interested in monsters since . . . well, forever."

Alexander nodded. "That sounds —"

"— dumb!" Rip barked. "We don't need your help, hoodie head!"

"Fine!" Nikki said. "But I've also figured out what S.S.M.P. stands for! And now I'm not going to tell you!" She marched into the girls' locker room.

"Forget about her," said Rip. "It's time for our fencing quiz!"

Alexander slapped his forehead. "The quiz is *today*?!"

Rip socked Alexander's arm as they walked into the boys' locker room.

12 FLOP QUIZ

Rip, how come you don't like Nikki?" Alexander asked.

"She's weird!" Rip slammed his locker shut. "She's always by herself, she wears that dopey hoodie . . . and now she's following us around!"

Rip looked at the floor. "But that's not the worst part."

Alexander raised an eyebrow. "No?"

"No, Salamander," Rip said. "Last week, that girl crossed the line. The lunch line. There was one dish of Jell-O left . . . and she took it! Right in front of me!"

Alexander laughed. "You're mad because of a little blob of Jell-O?"

Rip frowned. "It was strawberry."

Alexander and Rip walked into class, where students were taking practice swings with their foils. "Rip, you're wrong about Nikki. She's super smart. And brave — she doesn't let you push her around!"

"ALEXANDER BOPP!" shouted a froggy voice. "DEFEND YOURSELF!"

A laundry cart shot across the room, straight at Alexander.

Coach Gill stood atop the cart, sword held high.

"Wait, what?!" Alexander cried. He raised his practice foil.

Coach Gill did a backflip off the cart, and — **SMACK!** — swatted Alexander's foil from his hand.

"That was the quiz," she said, "and you *failed*!"

The coach leaned in close, pressing her cold face mask against Alexander's cheek. "You're as weak as Hoarsely," she croaked.

Alexander held his breath. *What was that about?* he thought.

"ALL RIGHT! WHO'S NEXT?" Coach Gill whirled around, bringing her sword down hard.

CLANK!

Her blade clashed against Rip's practice foil. Rip's grip was firm.

"Well done — you've been practicing." Coach Gill lowered her sword. "Rip Bonkowski, you're a model student!"

Rip blinked. Nobody had ever called him that before.

Coach Gill hacked her way down the line, giving everyone an F.

She shook her head. "Pathetic! Only one worthy opponent in the whole class!"

The coach stormed out of the gym.

Alexander dragged Rip over to Nikki, who was picking her foil up off the floor.

"You're right, Nikki," Alexander said. "We should team up. It's the only way to stop these tunnel fish. Right, Rip?"

He gave Rip a nudge.

"I'm, uh," Rip said, gritting his teeth. "I'm sorry you got mad when I called you names and stuff."

Nikki rolled her eyes. "Good enough," she said.

"Great!" said Alexander. "And now, Nikki, can you please tell us what S.S.M.P. stands for?"

"Tell you?" said Nikki. "Better yet, I'll show you! Meet me tonight at the old kickball diamond. 6:30, sharp!"

13 ON THE WRONG TRACK

CHOMP!

Alexander thought of hungry tunnel fish as he shoveled macaroni into his mouth.

"Mrmmh," he said, scooting his chair back.

"You're finished already?" his dad asked.

"Yeah, Dad." Alexander headed to the door. "I'm meeting my friends in ten minutes."

His dad gave a double thumbs-up. "Good for you, Al! Playing with your new friends . . . Call if you need anything!"

The sun was setting when Alexander arrived at the old kickball diamond.

"Hey, Salamander!"

Rip stood near home plate, talking to a girl Alexander hadn't seen before. She had a long ponytail and was holding a flashlight.

Alexander trotted over. "Hi, I'm Alexan —" He froze. "Wait. *Nikki*? Where's your hoodie?"

Nikki shrugged. "I only wear it during the day."

"Enough chitchat," Rip said. "Tell us what S.S.M.P. stands for!"

"Okay," said Nikki. "Follow me!"

She led the boys through the outfield, stopping near a stretch of rusty railroad track.

"Here we are!" Nikki said. She shone her flashlight on an old train car parked on the tracks — a caboose.

Alexander stared at the initials.

"*S.S.M.P.* is a *railroad*?"

"Yep," said Nikki. "It's the old Stermont Superfast Mountain Pacific Railroad. It stopped running years ago."

"What's a run-down railroad got to do with a monster notebook?" asked Rip.

"Beats me," said Alexander. "But there must be a connection! Let's peek inside and —"

BRUMBBUGGRUMMM!

"What's that noise?" Rip asked.

"Look!"
Nikki yelled. "The
pitcher's mound . . . It's *moving*!"

Just then, a spiky fin burst from the dirt. A scaly beast bulldozed its way toward the kids, chomping everything in its path.

"Run!" shouted Alexander.

14 HARD TO SWALLOW

The tunnel fish snapped at Alexander's heels. Then Nikki's. Then Rip's.

FLASH!

"A light!" Alexander called out. "Someone's in the caboose!"

They raced
over and climbed
onto the platform
at the back of the
caboose.

The tunnel
fish stopped at the
caboose's metal
wheels.

"Ha!" said Rip.
"End of the line,
sucker!"

The creature
opened its toothy
mouth.

RARRR!

A moment later, a school of growling tunnel fish began circling the caboose.

"Come on!" said Alexander, catching his breath. "We'll be safer inside."

He knocked on the caboose's back door. It swung open.

"Hello?" Alexander said. No answer.

Alexander stepped inside. A lantern hung from the ceiling, casting light on a strange yellow flag.

"Guys," Alexander said, "you've got to see what's in here."

The three of them inspected the caboose in total silence.

"Whoa," said Alexander, touching a map on the wall. "What *is* this place?"

"It's a hideout," said a whispery voice.

"Who said that?" Rip asked, looking around.

"It came from that box!" said Nikki, pointing to a large trunk in the corner.

CREEEAK!

The lid of the trunk opened, and Abraham Lincoln slowly rose from inside. Actually, it wasn't Abraham Lincoln. It was a tall, shaky man with a fake beard and top hat.

"Mr. Hoarsely?! What —" Alexander shouted.

"Shhh!" Mr. Hoarsely adjusted his beard. "I'm trying to hide!"

"From the tunnel fish?" asked Rip.

"Tunnel fish?" Mr. Hoarsely peered out the window. "Oh, no! *They're* here?! That means she's tracked me down!" He crouched back into the trunk, letting the lid close.

"*Who's* tracked you down?" asked Alexander.

SLAM! A white boot kicked in the door.

Coach Gill vaulted into the caboose. "AHA! I'VE FOUND YOU!" she shouted, drawing her sword. "REVENGE IS MINE! I — Wait…" She looked around. "Where's Hoarsely?"

Alexander shrugged. Rip and Nikki studied the floorboards.

"I know you're hiding him," Coach Gill hissed. "TAKE ME TO HIM — NOW!"

"Mr. Hoarsely?" asked Alexander, leaning against the trunk's lid. "Didn't you say he was on vacation?"

BRRHUGGHH!

A bone-rattling rumble shook the caboose, swinging the lantern and knocking a pair of skis onto Rip's head. Nikki stumbled, spilling a sack of giant feathers.

Alexander looked out the window in time to see an enormous fish explode through the soil! Its huge jaws chomped down on all of the surrounding tunnel fish — and the caboose — in one bite.

Alexander gulped.
So did the giant fish.

15 SLIP OF THE TONGUE

The caboose tumbled about, sending the trunk, papers, binoculars, and a saxophone flying off the shelves before stopping with a **SQUISH!**

"Everyone okay?" Alexander asked.

Rip and Nikki were on the floor. Mr. Hoarsely's trunk was upside down. And Coach Gill was tangled up in a hammock.

Alexander scrambled to a ladder on the wall. "Quick, to the roof!"

The kids climbed to the caboose's rooftop. But instead of seeing the starry night sky, they were greeted by slimy bits of whatever the tunnel fish had eaten for lunch.

"Okay, guys," said Alexander. "Any second now, Coach Gill will cut her way out of that hammock. We're surrounded by small angry tunnel fish, trapped inside the mouth of a giant tunnel fish, and about to be swallowed down into its stomach."

S.S.M.B.

"Then I say, let's go down fighting!" said Nikki.
Rip, for once, smiled at Nikki.

"Good," said Alexander, checking his pockets.
"What do we have to defend ourselves with?"

WHO HAS THE BEST WEAPON?

Alexander: A yo-yo!

Rip: A ski pole!

Nikki: A giant feather!

Answer: Nobody. These are all lousy ways to protect
yourself from a fish monster attack.

"ENOUGH!" Coach Gill gurgled. She sprung up to the roof, leveling her sword at Alexander. "You've ruined *everything*! After all these years, I was about to destroy the S.S.M.P.!"

"The railroad?" asked Rip.

"No, shrimp brain! S.S.M.P. stands for Super Secret Monster Patrol!"

"So *that's* what it stands for!" said Alexander.

Coach Gill groaned. "And now that I'm stuck in a stupid fish's mouth, I'll *never* get Hoarsely!"

She removed her mask and cut away her armor.

Alexander's jaw dropped. "You're a tunnel fish?" he asked.

"Don't insult me!" said Coach Gill. "Tunnel fish are *beasts*. They obey *me*! I'm a FISH-KABOB!"

The kids took a step back. Coach Gill raised her blade and — **POP!** — she snapped it onto a little opening on her face.

"ALEXANDER BOPP, DEFEND YOURSELF!"
Coach Gill lunged at Alexander, nose-first.
CLACK!
Rip blocked her attack with his ski pole.

"Good save, Rip!" yelled Alexander.

Rip grinned. "Stand back, guys. I've got this."

Coach Gill took a jab at Rip.

"I can't believe I'm fencing with a monster!" Rip said, blocking another thrust.

"We're not fencing . . ." said Coach Gill, ". . . we're sword-fighting!"

"HEE-YAARRGGHH!" Rip let out a battle cry and charged at the fish-kabob. She stepped aside. Rip crashed into his friends, and they all fell off the caboose. They landed on a giant bumpy green tongue, surrounded by growling tunnel fish.

Coach Gill looked down from the roof and laughed. Then she whistled to the small angry tunnel fish. "Dinnertime, my little chums!"

Alexander, Rip, and Nikki stood back-to-back-to-back as the small angry tunnel fish closed in.

Suddenly, Alexander felt his socks getting wet. The giant fish's mouth was filling with a murky fluid.

"Gross!" said Rip.

"It's only fish spit," said Nikki.

The small angry tunnel fish stopped advancing and looked up at Coach Gill. "Keep going!" she commanded. "Eat them! EAT!"

SLUURGHHH!

The ground buckled. The giant tunnel fish mashed its tongue against the roof of its mouth, squeezing the children and knocking Coach Gill off the caboose.

The tunnel fish crowded around Coach Gill, whimpering.

Alexander got to his knees. "Look! They're afraid!"

"Afraid of what?" asked Nikki.

A wave of slobber flooded the giant fish mouth.

"Of getting swallowed down into the giant fish's belly!" yelled Alexander.

16 BLAAARF!

W hat do we do?" Rip gasped.

Alexander looked at the yo-yo in his hand: *It's awesome to floss 'em.*

He gave the yo-yo a hard spin outward, and — CLONK! — yanked down, wedging it between two giant teeth.

"Grab on!" Alexander cried. He held fast to the yo-yo as Rip and Nikki hugged his legs.

The fish gulped down its mouthful, washing Coach Gill and the small angry tunnel fish down its throat.

The kids and caboose stayed put.

"Holy mackerel," said Alexander. "It worked!"

"We're lucky your dad's a dentist!" said Nikki.

Rip wiped slime off his face. "Okay," he said, "we didn't get swallowed, but we're still stuck in a fish mouth!"

"Oh yeah?" said Nikki. "Watch this!" She wiggled the giant feather on the fish's tongue.

The tongue quivered for a second. Then —

BLAAARF!

The giant fish spewed the kids and caboose out onto dry land. Then it tunneled back into the ground.

"If the notebook's right, that giant tunnel fish should sleep for 99 years now," said Alexander. "I'm pretty sure eating Coach Gill and all of the other tunnel fish counts as a big meal."

The kids looked around. They were in the middle of a forest.

"Hey," said Rip. "We're in Gobbler's Woods. Look, Salamander, that's your house!"

CREAK!

Mr. Hoarsely climbed down from the caboose.

"First, it was the balloon goons," he moaned. "Then the worms, the tunnel fish, and a phone threat from a fish-kabob. I can't take it anymore! I quit!"

"Quit what?" Nikki asked.

"The Super Secret Monster Patrol," said Mr. Hoarsely. "Congratulations. You kids are in charge now. You've already got the notebook, and here's your headquarters." He nodded toward the drool-covered caboose. "Oh, you'll need this," he added. He handed Alexander a ripped sheet of notebook paper.

"But wait —" said Alexander.

"What about —" asked Rip.

"Where were —" began Nikki.

"Tut!" said Mr. Hoarsely. "I'm dizzy, cold, and up past my bedtime. Good luck battling the next monster, leap-year boy!" He looked into Alexander's eyes, and then staggered away.

Alexander held up the paper. "It's the missing page from the notebook!"

OFFICIAL
S.S.M.P. OATH

RAISE YOUR LEFT HAND AND REPEAT.
(By moonlight, if you can stay up late enough.)

When googly-eyed monsters all covered in ooze
start swallowing school children whole,
I swear that I'll fight 'em (and try not to lose)
by joining this secret patrol.

"An oath?" asked Nikki. "Should we all swear to it?"

"Yes," said Alexander. He held up his left hand. "Stermont is counting on us."

The three slimy friends recited the oath.

Then Alexander completed his first official task as leader of the Super Secret Monster Patrol: He added another monster to the notebook.

FISH-KABOB

A scaly monster with
a sword for a nose.

SILENCE! Fish-kabobs are bossy, especially to tunnel fish.

> **HABITAT** Hospital laundry rooms?

> **DIET** Tuna salad, from the smell of things.

> **BEHAVIOR** Fish-kabobs are master ~~sword-fighters~~ fencers. They can unscrew their sword-noses to disguise themselves as regular people.

> **WARNING!** Don't fight a fish-kabob unless you've had more than one fencing lesson!

THE NOTEBOOK OF DOOM

QUESTIONS & ACTIVITIES!

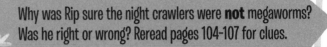

Why was Rip sure the night crawlers were **not** megaworms? Was he right or wrong? Reread pages 104-107 for clues.

Why are so many night crawlers coming above ground?

Look at pages 164-165. What items in the caboose help explain what the place is used for?

Do you think it is a good idea for Alexander and Rip to team up with Nikki? Why or why not? Use examples from the story to make your argument.

How do Alexander, Rip, and Nikki use their unlikely weapons to save themselves from the fish-kabob and the tunnel fish? Reread pages 174-182 for the answers!

scholastic.com/branches

TABLE OF CONTENTS

CHAPTER 1: CLEANUP CREW 191

CHAPTER 2: I SEE LONDON, I SEE FRANCE 198

CHAPTER 3: PHOTO NO-NO 205

CHAPTER 4: RED IN THE FACE 210

CHAPTER 5: OPEN WIDE 216

CHAPTER 6: IN THE DARK 221

CHAPTER 7: THE OTHER MONSTER 228

CHAPTER 8: FANGS FOR THE MEMORIES 233

CHAPTER 9: BRIGHT IDEA 239

CHAPTER 10: TOTALLY FLOORED 245

CHAPTER 11: SHADOW BOXING 249

CHAPTER 12: GOPHER DAY! 254

CHAPTER 13: THE HOLE STORY 259

CHAPTER 14: SKY'S THE LIMIT 264

CHAPTER 15: A TIGHT SPOT 270

CHAPTER 16: SPRING IN HER STEP 274

1 CLEANUP CREW

KER-SMASH!

The sixty-story slime creature knocked over another skyscraper.

"That's one scary monster, huh, Al?" said Alexander's dad.

Alexander Bopp yawned. "It's a neat comic, but I wouldn't call Swamp-Yak 'scary.'"

"Are you nuts?!" his dad said. "He's got seven eyes! And lightning breath!"

"Sorry, Dad," said Alexander. "But Swamp-Yak is silly. He slips on a bowling ball and falls into a volcano — THE END. A *real* monster would be way smarter than that."

Alexander's dad laughed. "Oh, Al. You take this monster stuff too seriously."

Alexander *was* serious about monsters, ever since he had moved to Stermont. The town was crawling with them. Real, scary monsters — not the kinds you find in comic books.

"All right, kiddo. You can go play outside," said Alexander's dad.

"Thanks, Dad!" Alexander yelled as he shot out the door and into the woods.

He followed a footpath to an old caboose. The train car was the hideout of the Super Secret Monster Patrol, which was also known as the S.S.M.P. The S.S.M.P. was a group of kids who fought monsters. This group had fallen apart years ago, but Alexander had restarted it after being attacked by monsters.

Alexander climbed into the caboose. There was stuff everywhere: papers, boxes, flashlights, ice skates, a saxophone, a birdcage, a globe, a cheese grater, and a basket of Ping-Pong balls. In other words, everything you might need to fight a monster.

In the middle of this mess sat Rip and Nikki, the only other members of the S.S.M.P.

"Sorry I'm late," said Alexander. "How's the cleanup going?"

"Great!" said Nikki. "I've been organizing all of our gear."

"And I drew this awesome picture of me fighting balloon goons at your leap-year birthday party," said Rip. "And look! Here's me sword-fighting the fish-kabob monster!"

"Sheesh!" Nikki said, whipping a Ping-Pong ball at Rip. "You didn't defeat those monsters single-handed, you know."

"Fine," he said. "I'll add you to the picture. And Salamander." Salamander was Alexander's nickname. He was *almost* used to it.

"Oh, and check this out!" Rip said. He tossed something curved and white to Alexander. It was a jawbone. With fangs.

Nikki's eyes grew wide.

Alexander studied the fangs.

Rip whistled. "Those are some serious choppers! This jawbone must have come from a super-evil monster!"

"Evil?" said Nikki, sinking into her hoodie.

Alexander snapped his fingers. "I *know* this monster!" he said.

Alexander unzipped his backpack and pulled out the official S.S.M.P. notebook. He had found it on his first day in Stermont. He never went anywhere without it.

Alexander thumbed through the monster-filled pages. "I remember seeing a long-toothed monster that —"

"NO!" Nikki shouted. She tore some pages from Alexander's notebook.

Then Nikki ran out of the caboose without saying a word.

Alexander closed the notebook. "What was *that* about?" he asked.

Rip shrugged.

"AL!" shouted a voice.

"Gotta run," said Alexander. "Dad's taking me shopping for clothes."

"Oh, yeah — tomorrow's picture day," said Rip. He flexed his arms. "I should practice my poses."

Alexander shook his head.

CHAPTER 2

I SEE LONDON, I SEE FRANCE

Alexander hiked up his pants and looked in the fitting-room mirror.

I look like a rodeo clown, thought Alexander.

His dad peeked in through the curtain and smiled. "Now *those* are some snappy slacks!"

Alexander groaned. "Can't we just buy the plain black suit?"

"Sure, Al. Suit yourself!" said his dad. "I'll go pick out some ties."

Alexander closed the curtain. Then he froze. Something in the mirror had moved. A cold draft tickled his back, as if someone had forgotten to close the fridge.

"Dad?" he asked, peeking over his shoulder. "Is that you?"

The curtain was still closed.

Alexander looked back at the mirror. His eyes were bugging out. His nose was twitching. And his mustache was drooping.

Mustache? Alexander blinked. Wait . . . it was just a shadow under his nose. The shadow wiggled.

It's swaying, he thought, *like the tail of a —* he gasped — *a giant snake!*

The shadowy snake slithered across the mirror, ready to strike.

"Ack!" Alexander leaped backward, right out of his pants. And right out of the fitting room. He crashed into a rack of belts.

"I found a tie," said Alexander's dad, strolling into view. He lowered an eyebrow.

Alexander looked down. A bright yellow cartoon crane smiled up at him. He was wearing his Stanley the Steam Shovel underpants — in the middle of the store. Alexander's knees wobbled. "I, um . . ."

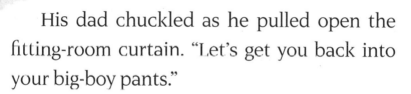

His dad chuckled as he pulled open the fitting-room curtain. "Let's get you back into your big-boy pants."

Alexander slowly stepped back inside. There was no sign of the snake shadow.

Did I see a monster? Alexander wondered. *Or was that snake-thing just a trick of the light?*

Alexander got dressed and followed his dad to the checkout counter. "Snakes . . . eels . . . a leech, maybe?" He muttered to himself as he flipped through the monster notebook.

SCREECH LEECH
A long purple three-eyed leech.

HABITAT

Found in closets.
(They blend in
with the belts
and neckties.)

KOO-RAWWK!

A screech leech's cry sounds like a duck playing a broken kazoo.

DIET > Chipmunks. Preferably with BBQ sauce.

BEHAVIOR > These bloodsuckers scream when they're hungry.

WARNING! > When you're near a closet, NEVER act like a chipmunk!

Alexander closed the notebook.

Could that thing in the fitting room have been a screech leech? he thought. *I'll have to see what Rip and Nikki think tomorrow at school.*

3 PHOTO NO-NO

$\mathbb{A}$lexander fiddled with his tie as he hurried to the old hospital.

Actually, it wasn't a hospital. It was where he went to school while the new Stermont Elementary building was being built. But today, as he stepped inside, he saw that it wasn't a hospital *or* a school. It was a cornfield.

A fake cornfield. There was a fake wooden fence, a fake wagon wheel, and a row of fake corn with a beautiful fake sunset.

There was even a fake scarecrow behind the camera. Wait. It wasn't a scarecrow: It was Mr. Hoarsely. To most kids, he was the school secretary, but Alexander, Rip, and Nikki knew him as a member of the original S.S.M.P.

"Alexander, you're late!" said Mr. Hoarsely.

Alexander's classmates were lined up behind the wagon wheel. Alexander wondered how long they'd been holding their poses.

"Uh, sorry," Alexander said. He took a spot between Rip and Nikki.

"About time, Salamander!" said Rip. He wore a clip-on tie, and it looked like someone had even tried to comb his hair this morning.

"Quiet down, please!" said Mr. Hoarsely.

"Guys," Alexander whispered, "I saw a monster yesterday!"

"Really? Cool!" said Rip.

"Oh," said Nikki. She hadn't dressed up for picture day.

"Um, Nikki?" said Alexander. "Is something wrong?"

Nikki pulled her hood down to her eyebrows. "I'm just not big on photos," she said.

"I hear you," said Rip. "It must be hard to be in a picture with a good-looking guy like me."

Nikki groaned.

"Smile, everyone," said Mr. Hoarsely.

Everyone smiled. Actually, not quite everyone.

"You, too, Nikki," said Mr. Hoarsely.

Nikki didn't smile.

Mr. Hoarsely sighed. "Maybe you could — *eep!*" He tripped on his tripod as a mean-looking woman pushed her way through the corn.

It was Principal Vanderpants.

"Nikki," she said. "Would you be so kind as to smile for one hundredth of a second, so Mr. Hoarsely can photograph your class?"

Nikki tightened her lips. She looked like she had swallowed a bug.

"No good," said Ms. Vanderpants, shaking her head. "Smile, Nikki!"

Nikki bared her teeth. Her smile was wide and bright. But two of her teeth were extra long. And pointy.

A second later, she snapped her mouth shut.

CLICK!

Alexander blinked.

CHAPTER 4

RED IN THE FACE

R ip! We *have* to talk!" said Alexander.

He ran to the lunch line, where Rip was getting a tray.

"Hey," said Rip. "Look! For once, I am not grossed out by lunch. Although I can't say I'm thrilled about the rest of the week."

"Forget the menu!" said Alexander. "Have you noticed anything strange . . . about Nikki?"

Rip took a plate of chicken fingers. "Like how she ripped those pages from the notebook yesterday?"

"No, not that," said Alexander. "Well, maybe that." He spoke quietly. "Nikki has *fangs*, Rip."

"Oh, geez!" said Rip, grinning. "There's no way Nikki's got fangs."

Alexander frowned. "But I saw —"

"Hey, guys," said Nikki, stepping in between them. "I saved us a spot."

Alexander followed Rip and Nikki to a table.

"So, Salamander," said Nikki. She punched a straw into a juice box. "Tell us about this monster you saw yesterday."

JUICE!

Alexander hadn't noticed it before, but Nikki barely moved her lips when she talked. He couldn't get a good look at her teeth.

"Well," he said. "I was trying on pants, when —"

"GROSS!" Rip yelled, pointing his chicken finger at Nikki. "What are you doing?"

BLOOP! BLOP!

Nikki was pouring tons of ketchup all over her plate.

"What?" she asked.

Rip made a face. "I was hoping to make it through lunch without gagging."

Nikki drowned a tiny nugget of chicken in her lake of ketchup. Then she ate it. A drop of red rolled down her chin.

Alexander stared at Nikki. "So . . . anyway. Maybe it was just a shadow, but I think I saw a snake monster. Or a leech."

"A leech?!" said Rip. "Bloodsucking monsters are the *worst*! With their fangs and —"

"ENOUGH!" Nikki shouted. She grabbed her juice box and — SPLISSHH! — sprayed Rip in the face. Then she stomped out of the cafeteria.

"What did I say?" asked Rip, dripping with cherry punch.

Alexander handed Rip a napkin. "I'm not sure," he said. "But you should probably wash up."

Rip headed to the bathroom. As Alexander nibbled a chicken finger, he noticed a strange shadow along one wall. It was shaped like a sledgehammer.

The hammer
shadow rose up
as Rip walked
by and then it
silently smashed
down — right onto
Rip's own shadow.

Rip shivered a
moment, but kept
walking.

Alexander
stopped chewing.

Rip's shadow had
sprouted antlers!

5 OPEN WIDE

During math class, Alexander checked the monster notebook. He found nothing about creepy animal-shaped shadows.

BRINNGGG!

As the final bell rang, Alexander hurried over to Rip's desk.

"What's up, Salamander?" Rip asked. "Does Nikki have tentacles now?"

"No!" said Alexander. "It's your shadow! It's turned into some kind of reindeer creature."

"What?" Rip said. He glanced at the wall. Rip's shadow was back to normal: no antlers.

He looked back at Alexander and cleared his throat. "Ahem."

"I don't understand!" said Alexander. "Your shadow was all wonky at lunch!"

Rip laughed. "Hey, Nikki!" he called. "Help me talk some sense into — Oh. She's gone already."

Alexander slouched. "Never mind, Rip. I should go, too. I'm meeting Dad at his office."

"All right," Rip said. "Watch for reindeer!"

Alexander's dad's office was only a few blocks from school, but the walk there felt like 100 miles.

I've only made two friends since moving here, thought Alexander, *and now they've got fangs and antlers! Am I going bananas?*

"Hello, kiddo," called a voice.

Alexander stopped at a sign reading BOPP DENTISTRY. His dad was kneeling behind the sign.

"My poor tulips," he said. "It's like they're not getting enough sunlight."

"Maybe they're being blocked by —" Alexander shuddered. A chill crept up his back. He saw his father's shadow stretch across the lawn. It was shaped like a T. rex.

"Dad!
Your shadow!"
Alexander yelled.
"It's a dinosaur!"
As Alexander's dad
stood up, his dino shadow
twisted back into a regular
people shadow.

"Oh, Al," he said. "It's just
the light. Haven't you seen
a shadow puppet before?"
He wove his fingers together.
"Look! A birdie!"

"I don't know, Dad," said
Alexander. "Your shadow
looked —" His eyes grew huge.
"Nikki? What are *you* doing here?"

Nikki came up the walk. "Oh, hi,
Salamander," she said. "I'm here to see
your dad."

"Howdy!" said Alexander's dad.

Nikki swallowed. "Uh, hi, Mr. Bopp. I was hoping you could help me with" — she shot Alexander a glance — "my teeth."

"Anything for a pal of Al's!" said Alexander's dad. "What exactly is the problem?"

Nikki closed her eyes and then opened her mouth wide.

Alexander's dad leaned in for a look. "Those are some serious choppers!" he said.

He turned back to Alexander. "Son, why don't you run home and start on your homework?"

"Ugh," said Alexander.

"Meanwhile, Nikki and I will head inside and see what we can do about her overbite."

He said "overbite," and not "fangs"! Maybe Nikki is normal after all, thought Alexander. *Not like that dino shadow!*

6 IN THE DARK

Good morning, early bird!" sang a chirpy voice. Alexander's teacher popped out of a hatch in the classroom wall.

Alexander sighed. "Hi, Mr. Plunkett."

"You're just in time to help," Mr. Plunkett said. He wheeled out an old machine that looked like a cross between a telescope and a toaster. "You'll be running the projector today."

Alexander fussed with the projector while the rest of the class arrived. Rip gave Alexander a slap on the back as he walked by. Alexander noticed Rip's shadow was Rip-shaped.

Then Nikki showed up. At least, she *looked* like Nikki. But she *seemed* like a totally different girl. She took long steps. She held her head high. And then, she smiled. It was a mile-wide, eyes-closed, stretch-your-cheeks kind of smile.

"Salamander!" Nikki stepped in front of the projector's beam. Alexander squinted as light reflected off the silver wires on her teeth. "I love love *love* my new braces!" she said. "Your dad's the best!"

Her teeth
seemed less pointy
with the braces. *How could I
have thought she was a monster?* thought
Alexander. Then he gasped.

Although Nikki stood directly in the light, she
had no shadow!

FLICK! Out went the lights. "Okay, class," Mr. Plunkett said. "What's special about tomorrow?"

"It's Gopher Day!" shouted everyone except Alexander.

Gopher Day? Alexander wondered.

"Yes, Gopher Day!" said Mr. Plunkett. "So instead of a boring old science lesson, we're going to watch a filmstrip today!"

Everyone cheered. Except Alexander, again.

"Mr. Bopp, start the film!"

Suddenly, a dark blur washed across the screen.

"Boooo!" the class shouted.

Alexander fiddled with some knobs, but the smudge wouldn't budge.

"Aw, nuts — show's over, folks!" said Mr. Plunkett, switching the lights back on. "Remember: Bring your families to Gopher Day!"

"And also," said Mr. Plunkett, waving a large envelope, "your pictures are ready." He handed out the photos.

Alexander stared at the class picture, wide-eyed. Right there, looming behind his classmates, were the monsters he'd been looking for.

7 THE OTHER MONSTER

Alexander sat alone on the low end of the teeter-totter. He took the folded note from his pocket and reread it.

EMERGENCY S.S.M.P. MEETING.
AFTER SCHOOL.
PLAYGROUND.
—RIP

Suddenly:

"Whoa!" Alexander found himself teetering three feet in the air. Rip had jumped onto the totter end.

"Okay, weenie," Rip said. "You were right about the shadow monsters."

Alexander held up the class photo. "They really ruined our picture, didn't they?"

"Picture, shmicture!" said Rip. "I'm talking about *me*! I got in trouble last night for staying up late. But I didn't do it!"

Rip took a step back. Alexander crashed to the ground.

"It was after bedtime," said Rip. "Mom was taking out the trash, and she thought she saw me through the curtains, dancing around — wearing antlers."

"You were dancing?" asked Alexander.

"No! I was asleep!" Rip barked. "My stupid reindeer shadow was dancing! But when Mom flipped on the light to yell at me, it was gone!"

Rip looked at Alexander. Alexander did not know what to say.

"So when did that shadow thing get me, anyhow?" asked Rip.

"Yesterday, after lunch," said Alexander. "The shadow smashed onto you when you were walking to the bathroom. And I have already checked the notebook — there's nothing about them in there."

"Hmm . . ." said Rip.

"Hey, guys!" Nikki trotted over. "*There* you are!"

Alexander smiled. "Nikki!"

"So get this, Nikki," said Rip. "Stermont is swarming with shadow smashers!"

"Oh, really . . ." said Nikki, jamming her hands into her hoodie pocket.

"Yeah!" said Alexander, "I've seen them all over town: in the fitting room, in our class photo, on my dad, and, um, on Rip. They even screwed up the Gopher Day filmstrip and my dad's tulips. We should —"

"Stop," said Nikki.

Alexander and Rip gave Nikki a puzzled look.

"We need to talk about *another* monster in Stermont," she said.

"Ugh," said Rip. "You mean we have to fight something *besides* shadow smashers?"

"I hope not," said Nikki. She looked at Alexander as she pulled the torn-out notebook pages from her pocket. "The other monster is *me*."

JAMPIRE

U mm . . ." Alexander was speechless.

"Poor Nikki," said Rip, shaking his head. "Sure, you're a weirdo. But a *monster*?!"

Nikki handed over the notebook pages. Alexander and Rip looked at the drawings and then at Nikki.

"This . . . is you?" asked Rip.

"Sort of," said Nikki. "But the entry was all wrong, so I fixed it." She took a roll of tape from her pocket. "Here, I'll put these pages back."

WRONG!

JAMPIRE

A terrible undead monster.

smart, brave girl.

HABITAT Graveyards.

Grade schools!

PEEK! Jampires have no shadows.

DIET > Blood? Yuck! No! Anything red and juicy: ketchup, fruit punch, raspberry jam, jelly donuts, strawberry gummies.

BEHAVIOR > Jampires are ~~evil.~~ friendly.

Also, they can see in the dark.

WARNING!

Keep jampires out of direct sunlight!

"So. Any questions about jampires?" said Nikki. "I'll tell you anything. But you've got to promise to keep my secret!"

"Cross my heart," said Alexander.

"And hope to die!" said Rip. He frowned. "No, wait. Hope to sprain my ankle!"

"Good enough," said Nikki.

"Okay," said Alexander. "Can you turn into a bat?"

Nikki rolled her eyes. "No. That's ridiculous."

"Or eat people's brains?" added Rip.

"Gross, no!" said Nikki. "It's mostly a lot of little things: like seeing in the dark, or getting sunburns in like five seconds."

"Or casting no shadow during the filmstrip," said Alexander. "You really are a ... uh ..."

"A monster," Rip mumbled.

"I wasn't going to tell you," said Nikki, "but then I lost my baby teeth and my fangs started  coming in. So I thought I should be honest with . . . you know, my best friends."

Again, Alexander was speechless.

But not Rip. "Thanks," he said, "for lying to us this whole time."

Nikki took a step back. "I didn't — I would *never* lie to you! I just —"

She rushed off the playground.

"Rip! Go easy on her!" said Alexander. "It was brave of Nikki to tell us her secret."

"Yeah," said Rip. "So when are you going to kick her out of the S.S.M.P.?"

Alexander's jaw dropped. "Huh?"

"We can't have a *monster* in the Super Secret *Monster* Patrol!" Rip said. "She's what we are supposed to be fighting!"

Alexander looked at Rip.

"It's your call, Salamander. You're the head of the club," said Rip.

"Um, can we talk about this tomorrow?" Alexander said.

"Fine," said Rip. "Let's meet at the caboose in the morning, since there's no school. What are you doing tonight, anyway?"

"It's board game night," said Alexander. "I should go."

H elp!" Alexander's dad shouted. "I'm being swallowed by a nine-armed space-blob!"

"Okay, Dad," said Alexander. He rolled a six and saved his dad.

Alexander's dad looked up from his cards. "Something tells me you're not into this game."

Alexander dumped his spaceships back in the box. "Sorry, Dad. It's been a rough day."

"Cheer up, Al," his dad said. "Tomorrow's Gopher Day!"

"Yeah," said Alexander. He gave his dad a hug and shuffled up to bed.

Alexander read the notebook for a while before finally turning off his flashlight. His bedroom went dark.

Maybe Rip's right. Maybe we should *kick Nikki out of the S.S.M.P.*, he thought. *But we're a team.*

He let out a long sigh. Then he gasped — he could see his breath! The room had suddenly become icy cold — just like that time in the fitting room.

A shadow smasher! He jolted upright. The dark shadow glided across a patch of moonlight on the wall.

Straight for his bed.

Alexander rolled to the floor. The shadow twisted into a sledgehammer, and — POW!

Alexander's feet felt all tingly. He looked back and saw that his shadow had grown into the shape of a giant spider.

The spider shadow followed him along a wall. Alexander scrambled toward the opposite corner of his room. CONK! — he bumped his night-light.

Suddenly, the spider shadow paused, all eight legs trembling.

Is it afraid of me? Alexander wondered, sitting up. *No, not me — it's the light! Just like how Rip's reindeer shadow disappeared when his mom turned on his bedroom light!*

Alexander kicked his nightstand. His flashlight fell off, rolling toward him. He pointed it at the shadow smasher and flicked the switch.

The spider shadow quivered in the light. Then it peeled away from Alexander's feet and dashed under the bed.

Alexander quickly dragged a lamp and a glow-in-the-dark sword over to the night-light. He made a circle of light and sat in the middle, on a nest made of blankets.

"Sorry, shadow smasher," Alexander said to the underside of his bed. "Looks like I'll be reading 'til sunrise." He opened the S.S.M.P. notebook.

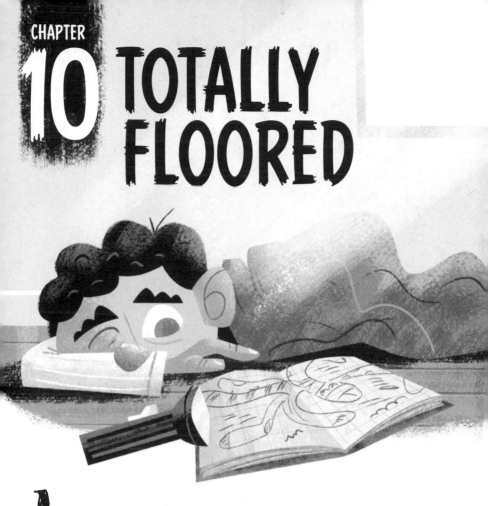

CHAPTER 10 TOTALLY FLOORED

Alexander woke up on the floor. His room was warm with sunlight, and there was no sign of the shadow smasher.

His now-dead flashlight lay near the open notebook....

SOCKTOPUS

A woven monster
with eight mismatched arms.

HABITAT

Dresser drawers.
Hampers.
Gym bags.

DIET

Sports socks.
knee-highs.
(No leg warmers.)

PEE-YEW! The stench of an unwashed socktopus can out-stink a skunk.

BEHAVIOR A socktopus is born when you forget to sort your socks. If you come across a single, unmatched sock, a socktopus is lurking nearby.

WARNING! The only way to stop a socktopus is to start wearing sandals.

Alexander closed the notebook and sat up. His shadow sat up, too.

"You're just my regular shadow, right?" said Alexander.

He did a little chicken dance. His shadow copied his funky moves exactly.

Alexander ran downstairs and gobbled up his breakfast in record time.

"Happy Gopher Day, Al!" his dad said. "You're going to the park with Rip, right?"

"Yep!" Alexander said. "See you there, Dad!" He shot out the door and into the woods. He couldn't wait to tell Rip about the spider shadow and the night-light.

A moment later, Alexander heard a scream coming from the caboose. ARRGH!

CHAPTER 11
SHADOW BOXING

Rip!" Alexander called, racing into the caboose. "What's going on?"

Rip was sitting on an overturned crate, rubbing his knuckles.

"Here's a tip, Salamander," Rip growled. "Don't try to punch your shadow."

Alexander spotted a fist-size dent in the wall. "Wait," he said, "why would you punch —"

"The shadow smashers got me, okay?!" Rip said, pointing to the floor. "Look!"

Rip now had the shadow of a very large, very cute, fluffy bunny.

Alexander tried not to smile.

"What a weenie shadow!" Rip yelled. "The reindeer was better."

Rip sat back, crossing his arms. His bunny shadow wiggled its ears. "So how do we get rid of these things?"

"I'll show you," Alexander said.

He grabbed a flashlight from the shelf and aimed it at Rip's heels. **CLICK!** Alexander blasted the bunny with light. The bunny shadow's whiskers twitched.

Then the bunny shadow peeled itself away from Rip's feet. It was trapped between the flashlight and a sunbeam.

Alexander tossed the flashlight to Rip. "All right, bunny," he said. "Tell us your evil plan, or my friend here will zap you with the light."

The shadow smasher shrugged.

"Okay," said Alexander. "Why do you smash people's shadows?"

The bunny made nibbling motions.

"You eat shadows?"

The bunny nodded.

"You're eating *my* shadow?!" Rip yelled.

The bunny shook its head.

"You're *not* eating his shadow?" asked Alexander. "Why not?"

The bunny marched in place.

"To walk?" Alexander rubbed his chin. "You're attaching to Rip so you can go somewhere?"

The bunny nodded.

"Are all of you shadow smashers going to the same place? Somewhere in Stermont?"

The bunny nodded. Then it twisted itself into the shape of a tree.

"You're all coming here, to these woods?" guessed Alexander.

"No — to Derwood Park!" Rip shouted. "The shadow smashers must want to wreck Gopher Day! Everyone will be there!"

The bunny nodded.

Rip checked a clock on the caboose's wall. "Gopher Day starts at noon! That's in twenty minutes! We've got to get over there!"

Even though it was a sunny day, Alexander grabbed every flashlight he could find.

"Hang on!" said Rip. "What are we going to do about Nikki?"

"That will have to wait," Alexander said. "Stermont needs us!"

The boys shot out of the caboose, leaving the bunny in their dust.

Derwood Park
was packed with
balloons, snacks,
and people.

"Wow! Gopher Day is a
big deal," said Alexander.

"I know," Rip said. "The whole town shuts down for this thing. If you ask me —" He looked back at Alexander, who had stopped in the middle of the crowd. "What?" he asked.

"Look," Alexander said, nodding toward the sidewalk.

Rip looked down. The people walking by were casting strange shadows. Some had horns, some had wings, some had tentacles. But none of the shadows looked human.

"It's crazy how nobody seems upset by their weird shadows," said Alexander.

"But wait! Look over there!" said Rip. "That kid with the camel shadow is going nuts!"

The boy was trying to point out a shadow smasher to his mom. She didn't seem interested, even when the camel shadow did a handstand.

Just then, two shoes stepped into view — with no shadow.

"Nikki!" said Alexander, looking up. He glanced at Rip, who glared back.

"I'm glad I found you guys," said Nikki.

"Not *now*!" Rip shouted. "One monster at a time! We'll handle the shadow smashers, and *then* we'll kick you out — I mean we'll talk — I mean . . . um . . . Salamander?"

Nikki looked at Alexander. "What's he talking about?"

Alexander sighed. "Nikki, we feel awful about this, but as members of the Super Secret *Monster* Patrol, we have, I guess, a duty to . . . That is . . ."

"Wait!" Nikki laughed. "Are you kicking me out of the S.S.M.P.?"

"Um," said Alexander. "I, uh . . ."

"Well, that's just perfect," said Nikki. "Because I actually came by to tell you I QUIT!"

The boys' mouths fell open.

"Oh, please!" said Nikki. "The S.S.M.P. fights monsters! Monsters like, oh, I don't know . . . ME! I don't want to be in your stupid monster-hating club anyway!"

Alexander frowned. "But —"

"Yeah, yeah," Rip said. "It's a real stake through the heart. Now let's *go*, Salamander!"

"Well, good!" said Nikki. She spun on her heels and disappeared into the crowd.

Before Alexander could say anything, he felt a jerk at his arm. "It's almost noon," said Rip, "and I think I know where the shadow smashers will strike!"

13 THE HOLE STORY

$\mathbf{A}$lexander and Rip squeezed through the balloon-holding, song-singing, pretzel-eating crowd of people with strange shadows. The boys soon found themselves near a bandstand.

A brass band honked its way through "You Are My Sunshine." The bandleader had a familiar shock of white hair.

"It's Mr. Hoarsely!" said Alexander.

"Never mind him," said Rip. "Check out the gopher hole."

There was a sign in front of the bandstand:

The sign pointed to a hole in the ground.

"Now everyone is just waiting for Stella to pop out," said Rip. "If she doesn't see her shadow, it means we'll have an awesome spring."

"Gopher Day sounds just like Groundhog Day," said Alexander.

"What? NO!" Rip shouted. "Oh, wait. Maybe."

Rip leaned in and whispered. "But I think Gopher Day is totally rigged! She *never* sees her shadow!"

The band played a loud "TA-DAAA!"

"Here we go!" said Rip.

Alexander scanned the crowd. The shadow smashers were pulling away from everyone's feet. They hopped from shadow to shadow until they reached the edges of the park.

Everyone's shadows were back to normal.

"I don't get it," said Rip. "Why did the shadow smashers all leave?"

The crowd grew silent as Stella peeped out of her hole. She ran into the open. Then she sat on the ground and scratched her ear.

The audience cheered.

"Hooray!" said a man in a gopher hat. "Stella didn't see her shadow! Sunny days are on the way!"

Just then, the air grew as cold as winter. From all corners of the park, shadow smashers melted together and stretched upward, totally blocking out the sun. The daytime sky became entirely dark — like the darkest night, with no stars.

Alexander could
see his breath as he spoke. "We're
too late. The shadow smashers have
made a shadow dome over Stermont!"

Stella squeaked as she
looked up at the darkened
sky. Then she scampered
back into her
hole.

14 SKY'S THE LIMIT

Despite the totally dark sky at noon on the first day of spring, the adults in the crowd were chatting happily. The kids, however, were starting to lose it.

ADULTS

HOW ODD!

IT'S LIKE A THUNDERSTORM, MINUS THE THUNDER!

KIDS

AAAAUGGHH!!

MOMMY!

"What's with these grown-ups?" Alexander asked. "It's like they don't see what's going on. Except for Mr. Hoarsely."

The boys
watched as he
dove behind a huge
spotlight near the
bandstand.

"It's getting even darker!"
said Rip. "I can't see the edge
of the park!"

Alexander gave Rip a couple of flashlights.
"Let's try to light up the sky!"

The boys ran around, waving their flashlights at the shadow dome.

The sky began to grumble.

"Is it working?" asked Rip.

"I'm not sure," said Alexander, "Maybe we could —"

"Hey, Al!" chirped a voice. Alexander's dad jumped out from the darkness. "Boy, Gopher Day is — hey, are you playing flashlight tag?"

Alexander glanced at Rip. "Uh, actually, Dad —"

"Swell!" said Alexander's dad. "Here, give me a flashlight." He closed his eyes and began counting to 100.

Rip and Alexander both
rolled their eyes.

"Okay, Rip," said Alexander,
"let's aim for the exact same spot."

Rip pointed his flashlight straight up.
Alexander angled his to match.

This time, the sky grumbled much louder.

"GIVE UP!"

A loud voice thundered from the sky.

Alone, the shadow smashers had been silent.

But together, they spoke in a booming voice.

"WE HAVE ALL
COME TOGETHER
TO BLANKET STERMONT IN
ETERNAL DARKNESS!"

The rumbling grew louder yet, and the sky became even darker. Now the flashlights only seemed to shine a few feet in front of them.

"It's no use," said Rip. "Our lights are too weak."

"IT WILL ALWAYS BE PAST YOUR BEDTIME! AND STERMONT WILL BE OURS!"

"All right, we get it, shadow smashers," growled Rip. "You're scary monsters who want us gone."

"STERMONT WILL BE DARK AND WINTERY ALL YEAR LONG! NO TREES! NO FLOWERS! AND CERTAINLY NO PEOPLE!"

Alexander lowered his flashlight. "The two of us are no match for a gazillion shadow smashers."

Then he felt a tap on his shoulder. "No, but the *three* of us might be."

Nikki stepped out of the gloom.

"Nikki!" said Alexander. "You came back?"

Even Rip seemed happy to see her.

"Yep," said Nikki, flipping her hood off her head. "I took an oath to protect my town, and I intend to keep it. Now all we need is a plan!"

15 A TIGHT SPOT

Since moving to Stermont, Alexander had been yelled at by bullies, teachers, and monsters. But getting yelled at by the sky was another thing altogether.

"FEAR US, SUN LOVERS! WE ARE NOW ONE POWERFUL SHADOW!"

Alexander's eyes brightened. "That's it!"

He whispered to his friends. A moment later, the three of them split up.

It was getting darker by the second. Alexander could no longer see his feet. He carefully made his way over to the gopher hole.

"Hey, smashers!" Alexander shouted, waving to the sky. "A little bunny told me you love to snack on shadows . . . especially bold, juicy shadows like mine! Check it out!"

CLUNK!

Rip switched on the spotlight, bathing Alexander in white light. His long, dark shadow cut across the park.

KA-BLASH!

There was a peal of thunder as the shadow smashers in the sky licked their chops.

"TURN OFF THAT LIGHT!!"

They all barreled down toward Alexander.

CHAPTER 16

SPRING IN HER STEP

N ow!" shouted Alexander.

He dove out of the way as Nikki sprang from behind the bandstand. She quickly took his place near the gopher hole. Rip held the spotlight steady, shining the light directly onto Nikki. Even standing in the powerful spotlight's beam, she cast no shadow. Nikki closed her eyes and gritted her teeth.

275

The first shadow smashed onto the ground behind her, fixing itself to her heels.

It looked over at Alexander and blinked.

GORAARRRGHH!!

With a terrible moan, a gazillion more shadow missiles rained down on that exact spot. Nikki didn't move. Over and over, the shadows smashed against one another, becoming darker and blurrier.

The sky became instantly sunny. As Alexander shielded his eyes from the brightness, he noticed several things:

1. Gopher Day was back in full swing.

2. Both Stella and Mr. Hoarsely were crawling out of their hiding spots.

3. Alexander's dad had made it to "87-Mississippi," and was still counting.

4. Nikki now had her own honest-to-goodness shadow.

"This is so cool," said Nikki. She skipped around, watching her new shadow move with her. "Did it work? Are they really trapped?"

"Well, that first shadow smasher looked confused when it got stuck to your heels, since you had no shadow for it to take over. Then the rest of them did what they do best: smash!" said Alexander. "By the time they all smashed together, they must've flattened themselves into one plain old shadow. Or something."

Rip ran over and offered a fist bump. "Nikki!" he hollered. "You rule!" He turned to Alexander. "I can't believe you wanted to kick her out of the S.S.M.P.!"

Alexander fake-punched Rip's arm.

"You know," said Alexander. "We three are running the show now, so we get to make up some new rules from time to time!" He flipped open the notebook and wrote on the inside cover:

RULE #1: NOT ALL MONSTERS ARE BAD.

Alexander smiled at Nikki. "Rip and I may not be jampires, and you may not be human, but who cares?! What matters is that we stick together. Nikki, will you please rejoin the Super Secret Monster Patrol?"

Nikki looked a little sunburned. Or maybe she was blushing.

"Of course I will," she said. "But first, add the shadow smashers to the notebook!"

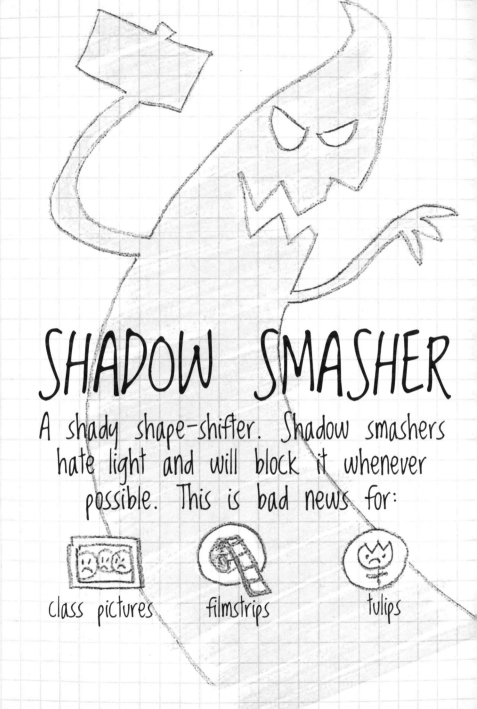

SHADOW SMASHER

A shady shape-shifter. Shadow smashers hate light and will block it whenever possible. This is bad news for:

class pictures   filmstrips   tulips

BRRRR! Shadow smashers bring a chill to the air.

> HABITAT Right behind you.

> DIET They "attach" to people and slowly eat their shadows.

> BEHAVIOR Shadow smashers travel by jumping from shadow to shadow.

> WARNING! Individual shadow smashers are silent. But put 'em together, and they

ROAR!

THE NOTEBOOK OF DOOM

QUESTIONS & ACTIVITIES!

What does *S.S.M.P.* stand for? What does the S.S.M.P. do? And who are the members?

Look at pages 234 and 235. What are the **differences** between the old description of the jampire and Nikki's new description?

Why does Rip want to kick Nikki out of the S.S.M.P.? Do you think he is right or wrong?

How does Alexander figure out what scares the shadow smashers? Reread Chapter 9 for clues.

Look at the filmstrip on pages 224-225. Now make your own filmstrip! Include the major events from this story. Use descriptive verbs like *groaned, scrambled, wiggled,* and *quivered.*

TROY CUMMINGS

has no tail, no wings, no fangs, no claws, and only one head. As a kid, he believed that monsters might really exist. Today, he's sure of it.

BEHAVIOR This creature tromps around until way past midnight, writing books, designing jigsaw puzzles, and drawing birthday cards.

HABITAT Troy Cummings lives in Greencastle, Indiana, with his wife and hatchlings.

DIET Malted milk balls.

EVIDENCE Few people believe that Troy Cummings is real. The only proof we have is that he supposedly wrote and illustrated The Eensy Weensy Spider Freaks Out! and Giddy-up, Daddy!

THE NOTEBOOK OF DOOM

READ ALL OF THE S.S.M.P.'S ADVENTURES!

More books coming soon!